Kreid raised his sword high above his head.

"Your quest has ended, Nightshade," he hissed. *"Prepare to die!"*

He brought down the weapon in a final savage strike.

Finding a last reserve of strength, Leandor half rolled, half fell to one side.

He glimpsed Kreid's face. A look of naked terror flashed across it as he realized his razor-sharp blade would not meet flesh. Unstoppable, it plunged toward the very thing he was created to protect.

It struck the book.

Also in the Point Fantasy series:

Doom Sword
Star Warriors
Peter Beere

Brog the Stoop
Joe Boyle

Firefly Dreams
The Webbed Hand
Jenny Jones

Renegades series:
Healer's Quest
Fire Wars
Return of the Wizard
Jessica Palmer

Wild Magic
Wolf-Speaker
The Emperor Mage
Realms of the Gods
Tamora Pierce

Elfgift
Foiling the Dragon
Susan Price

Enchanted Chronicles:
Dragonsbane
Dragon Search
Patricia C. Wrede

Point Fantasy

Stan Nicholls

SCHOLASTIC

Scholastic Children's Books
Commonwealth House, 1–19 New Oxford Street,
London WC1A 1NU, UK
a division of Scholastic Ltd
London ~ New York ~ Toronto ~ Sydney ~ Auckland

First published by Scholastic Ltd, 1996

ISBN 0 590 13272 5

Typeset by TW Typesetting, Midsomer Norton, Avon
Printed by Cox & Wyman Ltd, Reading, Berks.

10 9 8 7 6 5 4 3 2

For David Gemmell, the undisputed King

PRELUDE

In the beginning...

They were four in number.

They were strong, well-armed and ruthless. They were the elite of the Brotherhood of Assassins, experts in the craft of murder, the finest killers gold could buy.

They had planned their ambush to the smallest detail. They had the advantage of surprise and were cloaked by darkness.

They were aware of Dalveen Leandor's reputation but not unduly troubled by it. They knew he would be alone and that he was, after all, only a man. They saw no reason to fear him.

They didn't stand a chance.

*   *   *

The sorcerer raised the jewelled goblet and drank deep.

A trickle of the warm, sticky liquid seeped from the corner of his lip. He wiped it with the back of a bony hand. But some of the blood matted his black goatee beard.

Tossing aside the empty cup, he turned to a pedestal littered with sheets of yellowing parchment, weighted by a stack of crumbling books. The uppermost volume lay open, and he gazed intently at the strange, long-forgotten language covering its brittle pages. His dark eyes flared greedily at the thought of the knowledge they promised.

A scattering of black candles was the only source of light. They cast flickering shadows against the rough granite walls. The stone floor, polished smooth by generations of use, was covered in chalked and painted symbols.

Symbols of magical power, already ancient when the world was young.

The wizard dropped powdered incense into a brazier of glowing coals. Heady perfume filled the dank air. He took up the ceremonial sword, its silver blade carved with arcane runes, and made ready to enact the terrible rite.

His inner sanctum was in the highest tower of the fortress, and as he began to chant the words of the ritual, he glanced at its narrow window.

A deathly cold moon hung in the night sky.

* * *

Moonlight shimmered in puddles left by a recent fall of rain.

The young man strode along a deserted alley in the shadow of Torpoint's mighty wall.

His clothing was black. His hair, wound in a ponytail, was the same colour as his garb. His eyes were of like hue. His sole weapon was a sword in a leather scabbard at his waist, and he wore no armour or helm.

He moved with an easy confidence. But ever watchful, always alert.

The assassins heeded the sound of his footfalls on the glistening cobblestones and stiffened in their hiding places. All were dressed simply in uniform grey, and they were hooded. Attire favoured by those who walk the night with death in their hearts.

As he reached the alley's halfway point, where the gloom was deepest, two of the killers stepped out and blocked his path. The others slid from the darkness behind him to bar his retreat.

The young man showed no terror. He did not even seem surprised. Standing motionless, he silently regarded the brigands with eyes as chill as the dead moon above.

The larger of the two men before him took a pace forward. As sign of his status as leader he sported a waist-length cape trimmed with white wolf fur. This he flung back over his shoulders, revealing a sheathed sword. His hand caressed the weapon's hilt.

"Your hour of reckoning has come," he growled.

His companions drew daggers.

If they expected the young man to cry for help, or beg, or try to flee, they were cheated. He did not speak. Instead he slowly folded his arms and greeted the threat with an expression of contempt.

The leader frowned ominously, pulled free his sword and hissed, "Prepare to die, Nightshade!"

The young man smiled. He appeared amused.

Anger twisted the leader's face. His sword came up. The others edged closer, knives held out.

Something stirred deep in their intended victim's breast. It was a feeling he knew well. He expected it, and welcomed it. It was warm and intense.

And dreadful.

The assassins moved in, moonlight glinting on their blades.

Blood pounded through the young man's veins. A red haze filled his vision. Frenzy raged within him like a beast, demanding to be let loose.

He surrendered to it.

Droplets of sweat beaded the magician's forehead as he poured every iota of his concentration into the rite.

He followed the ritual carefully. He touched the tip of his ceremonial sword against the painted symbols in exactly the right order. He recited the words with precision.

Yet he was beginning to realize the spell wouldn't work.

He tried to hold down his temper, to curb the disappointment at failing once again.

His power was already great, but still not strong enough to achieve his ambitions, and he was impatient. But to gain the additional power he craved meant raising … them. And even he lacked the skill for such a task.

He glared at the pile of ancient volumes. They were useless for his purpose. Only the *book held the knowledge he needed; the secret that would allow him to pierce the veil separating this world from the dimension they inhabited.*

The book was the key to letting them in.

Despite the instinct that told him it would not succeed, he decided to carry the ritual to its conclusion. He focused his will.

And took comfort in the thought that at least one potential enemy would trouble him no more when this night was done.

The screaming had ended.

Four bodies littered the alley. Three dead, one mortally wounded.

Blinking the crimson mist from his eyes, Leandor calmly re-sheathed his sword.

He had dealt with the chief assassin in a way

that would not prove immediately fatal. As leader, he knew who ordered the ambush, and in the last few moments of his life would be made to give up the name.

The youthful warrior they called Nightshade moved to the groaning figure and knelt beside him. He noticed that the white fur trim of the man's cape was splashed with red. His breath was laboured, his eyes glazed. There was little time.

"You're dying," Leandor said.

"Tell me ... something ... I ... don't know," the leader rasped.

"That's what you're going to do for me. Who paid for my death?"

"I'll ... go to ... hell ... first."

"No doubt I'll see you there. Now answer the question."

Blood welled from the side of the man's mouth. He grew more ashen. *"Never, damn ... you. Can't ... can't make ... me ... talk..."*

Nightshade reached for a dagger lying by an assassin's body. He employed it with practised skill.

The leader talked.

And died soon after.

The name he heard confirmed Leandor's suspicion. Now the King must be told without delay.

He left the corpses for the night watch and hurried to the palace.

* * *

The only door to the tower's chamber was made of stout wood and heavily bolted. But it quickly shattered under the impact of many burly shoulders.

Dalveen Leandor, Captain of the Royal Guard and King's Champion, swept in with a company of armed militia. Absorbed by the ritual he was performing, the magician was taken unawares. The ceremonial sword fell from his hand and clattered to the floor.

"Nightshade!" he exclaimed.

"Surprised to see me, Avoch-Dar?"

The sorcerer raised his hands. But the soldiers moved swiftly to seize him before he could cast a spell.

"This is an outrage!" the wizard stormed. "I demand to see the King!"

"You shall have your wish," Leandor told him. "You're to be brought before him accused of treachery and attempted murder." He looked about the room, adding, "And I imagine there'll be a charge of practising unlawful magic, too."

Avoch-Dar fixed him with a menacing stare. "You'll regret this," he said darkly.

Leandor met his gaze and made no reply. Then he turned to an officer of the guard and nodded.

The magician was dragged away.

There was an air of expectancy in Torpoint's Great Hall.

The vast space held an assemblage of courtiers,

guards, servants, counsellors and sundry other functionaries. They stood quietly, awaiting their monarch's word.

Delgarvo's ruler, King Eldrick of the Lance, sat upon his raised throne in stern contemplation. He was of advanced age, his beard pure white, but half a lifetime spent as a warrior defending the realm had tempered him, as fire tempers steel. His bearing and form would not disgrace many a younger man.

Yet this day his face showed the years. It was plain that the decision he had to make was troubling him.

His daughter, Princess Bethan, was seated at his side. Fair and blue-eyed, she was a young woman of graceful beauty.

Dalveen Leandor, standing by her, seemed all the more striking in comparison. He wore his usual dark apparel that matched his olive eyes and raven hair. And where she was outgoing and open, he had a brooding nature.

As ever, Eldrick's closest confidant, Golcar Quixwood, was at his right hand. Commander of the Palace Guard, and a valued general in times of war, he was near the King's age, but still fit and muscular despite his greying beard and thickening waist.

All looked to the accused.

The wizard was on his knees before the throne,

his arms bound with chains of iron. Though the indignity did not quite wipe the arrogance from his features.

At length, the King spoke, his clear, strong voice filling the hall.

"The evidence is damning, Avoch-Dar. You have plotted against me and planned to take my place as sovereign. To clear your way to power, you ordered the murder of my Champion." He glanced briefly at Leandor. "And there is proof that you have delved into the realms of black sorcery, as forbidden by law."

Disapproving whispers rose from the crowd. The Royal Usher stopped them with a sharp rap of his staff against the marble floor.

"You have remained silent throughout these proceedings," King Eldrick continued. "Have you nothing to say in your defence?"

Avoch-Dar made no reply.

"We note that you do not deny your crimes." The monarch sighed. "Very well, I will give my judgement, though it grieves me to do so. I made you Court Magician because I trusted you, and you abused that trust. There can be no other verdict than guilty."

The sorcerer kept his surly gaze upon the King.

Eldrick addressed the hall. "Do any here disagree with my finding?"

None did.

"Then all that remains is to pass sentence." He looked down at the prisoner. "My will is that you are to be immediately banished to the barren wastes of Vaynor and live out the rest of your days there. Any attempt to escape exile carries the penalty of death. Do you understand?"

The magician spoke at last, his words sinister in tone. "I understand well enough," he snapped. "I understand that you're a fool, and as weak a ruler as I always suspected."

There were gasps from the gathered throng, shocked at so open a show of disrespect.

"If you are feeble enough to spare my life, then so be it," he went on. "I would not be so lenient were our positions reversed. But know this, Eldrick; you'll rue the day you let me live. For I vow the time will come when *you* will be at *my* mercy. And on *that* day you need expect no quarter." His flinty eyes darted to Leandor. "As for you, Nightshade, know that I have marked you for your meddling, and my revenge will be especially severe."

The King rose, his face flushed with anger. "Let the punishment be carried out!" he ordered.

Guards came forward and hauled the struggling sorcerer to the door.

His vile curses echoed through the hushed hall.

King Eldrick, his daughter, his oldest friend and his Champion sat pondering recent events in the now empty room.

Princess Bethan shuddered. "It was horrible, father. My spine chilled when Avoch-Dar swore revenge on you and Dalveen. And his *face*..."

"Have no fear," the King soothed, "he cannot harm us. He'll be taken to Vaynor at first light under heavy guard."

"And good riddance," Golcar Quixwood announced bluntly. "I never liked the man, nor trusted him."

"I know," Eldrick said, "and I wish I'd heeded your opinion sooner." He turned to his Champion. "You have long had doubts about the wizard, too, Dalveen, but you've expressed no opinion on my judgement of him. Come, you know you can speak freely."

"In truth, sire, I think his punishment is not hard enough."

"Would you have me put him to death? I am not that harsh a ruler."

"But you might have imprisoned him here in Torpoint where we could keep an eye on him."

"He dealt in deception, and I would prefer not to have such around me, even under lock and key in the palace dungeons."

"Is that the only reason?"

"No. I cling to the belief that Avoch-Dar was not always evil, but has been corrupted by dabbling in the ways of dark magic."

"Why do you say that?" Bethan asked.

"For reasons you are too young to remember, but which Golcar no doubt clearly recalls."

"That I do," the old warrior replied sadly.

"The night of your birth, daughter," the King explained, "I had summoned here a number of mystics, seers and diviners. Avoch-Dar was among them. We were gathered in this very chamber when word came that your mother, my beloved Nerissa, had gone into labour. But my joy at your birth turned to despair when she fell prey to a fever." He paused as painful memories flooded back. "She died shortly before dawn."

The Princess leaned over and gently squeezed his hand.

Eldrick smiled at her and continued the tale. "Grief nearly destroyed me. I found comfort in you, my dear, and in the support and wise counsel of Avoch-Dar. That helped me through those terrible days."

"And the same night I was born," Bethan said, "Dalveen was brought to the palace."

"Yes," Golcar confirmed. "Then, as now, I was commander of your father's personal guard. When I came across Dalveen while on patrol, abandoned fresh born, I begged your father to give the orphan royal protection."

"Suspecting the gods may have played a part in this discovery, I gladly consented," the King recalled. "I also let it be known that henceforth Avoch-Dar would fulfil the role of Court Magician. It was a time of great changes and mixed emotions. So perhaps you can see how I felt when I discovered the sorcerer had betrayed me."

Leandor frowned. "My feeling is that he was never loyal in the first place, Your Majesty."

"I take Dalveen's point," Golcar said. "Avoch-Dar may have been good at one time and became contaminated by evil. Then again, he may always have been evil and simply good at putting on an act. Who knows? The important thing is that he's *dangerous*. A man who hires assassins and practises diabolical magic."

"And from tomorrow he will be on his way to a remote and inhospitable desert land where he can hurt no one," King Eldrick declared.

"With respect, sire," Leandor stated, "I hope you're right. Because if you're not, it could be that the next time we hear of the wizard the tidings will be far from happy."

In a matter of months, Leandor was proved correct.

Despite his exile to Vaynor, a barren wasteland far to the south, Avoch-Dar prospered in evil. He continued to walk the path of necromancy and black magic, greatly increasing his command of sorcery.

The wizard used his hell-sent talents to build an

empire of darkness. He was joined by depraved and wicked followers, men who resented the benign rule of King Eldrick and sought his overthrow. Their ranks were swelled with creatures that were not human, nightmare beings and hordes of the undead, summoned from the nether worlds by Avoch-Dar's loathsome skills.

Driven by a lust for power and revenge, he intended taking by might what he had failed to gain through treachery.

As his forces grew in strength they began to mount raids into Delgarvo. Meeting little resistance, they struck deeper, soon threatening the realm's very heartland.

For many years Delgarvo had known peace under Eldrick's benevolent guidance. It was the greatest trading centre of the known world. Its subjects lived free of tyranny or want. The capital, Allderhaven, was a seat of knowledge, with poets, artists, songsmiths and philosophers thronging its ancient streets. Culture and learning prospered at the court of Torpoint, the royal palace.

The menace from the south threatened all that.

As skirmishes turned to battles, Eldrick gathered together the largest number of men at arms seen in the land for generations. Dalveen Leandor was promoted to the rank of Commander. Postponing his coming wedding to Princess Bethan, he set out to confront the sorcerer's multitudes in a series of ever more bloody conflicts.

Yet Avoch-Dar soon stood at the head of a huge invading army on Delgarvo's borders.

The war had begun in earnest.

Death was all.

The battle between Light and Darkness had raged for three days and three nights. There was fearful carnage. The putrid stench of decaying corpses perfumed the air.

After fighting more savage than any he had ever known, Dalveen Leandor realized that the tide had begun to turn in favour of King Eldrick's forces. The remnants of Avoch-Dar's army were retreating. They remained mighty in numbers and fiendish wizardry, but they could not win.

However, the gods of war had been little kinder to Eldrick's warriors. Slaughter had taken its awful toll, and they too were cheated of success. Both sides had fought to a standstill.

The sorcerer's evil had been halted. It had not been conquered.

Seeing an opening in the enemy's ranks, Leandor led his elite band of mounted warriors, the Sabretooth Corps, in a last assault. He had caught sight of Avoch-Dar and believed he could reach him. His plan was to bring an end to the madness by plunging his blade into the magician's black heart.

If heart he had.

The price was heavy. Of all his company, only Leandor survived the charge, and even his horse was slaughtered.

In a berserk rage he threw himself at the diabolical bodyguard surrounding his foe, willing to die if it meant achieving his mission. His flashing sword and thrusting dagger cut deep into the hell-spawn's corrupt flesh. And they replied with spell-hardened steel, with fang and claw, and a fury born of the pit.

Blades clotted with gore, his body covered in scores of wounds, by some miracle he beat back the defenders.

The wizard lord stood haughty in a war chariot of ebony and gold, adorned with magical symbols picked out in precious gems. Wickedly barbed scythes jutted from the hubs of its wheels. A pair of massive plains lizards, pink-eyed albinos, strained and snorted in the harness.

Certain now that his life would soon be at an end, Leandor renewed the attack.

As he cut down any who blocked his path, he saw the sorcerer's hand rise. Instantly, the remaining protectors fell back and lowered their weapons. An unholy silence descended.

Champion and black magician locked gazes.

Avoch-Dar's eyes were dark pools of infinite foulness.

His scarlet cloak billowed in a gust of icy wind. He regarded Leandor with naked hatred and swiftly conjured a spell.

The young warrior all men knew as Nightshade

readied himself for some magical onslaught. He raised his sword.

And at that moment what felt like a gentle breeze caressed the arm he held aloft. It began to sting, grew numb, then felt as though it was bathed in fire. The increasing pain forced him to drop his sword. Yet none of the defenders rushed forward to take advantage of this, as he expected them to.

He sank to his knees in unspeakable agony, and watched bewildered as the arm twisted and spasmed.

His clenched fist turned pale. It took on the appearance of crystal.

Then crumbled to dust.

Fine grey ash poured from his silk sleeve as the rest of the limb dissolved and fell away.

Horrified and astonished, Leandor glimpsed the magician's cruel face as he slumped to the ground. His one thought as he sank into a bottomless well of darkness was that he would not wake again in this world.

But Avoch-Dar did not kill him.

The sorcerer preferred the idea of humiliating Leandor, of letting him suffer for a while in his maimed state before taking his life. And he was sure that day would arrive soon.

Now, though, his magical powers were drained and he had lost too many of his warriors to continue the fight.

He withdrew from the battlefield and took his army back to the safety of Vaynor.

Hours later, when Leandor regained consciousness, he was delirious and near insane.

His pride, as well as his body, was deeply injured. He had never lost in combat before and felt ashamed. Ashamed for failing, for allowing himself to be bested by a spell because he had mistaken recklessness for bravery.

The legend of Nightshade was fed by numerous stories of what happened that day.

Many assumed Dalveen Leandor had died on the field of battle.

Others said they saw him in the chaos, lacking an arm and stumbling across the numberless dead.

Some swore he found a stray horse and fled.

And that the sky wept blood.

Chapter 1

Life was returning.

The tree had started to bud.

A single leaf grew at the end of an otherwise bare branch, a splash of yellow green swaying gently in the constant wind.

The hermit, sitting cross-legged beneath, meditated upon it.

Unmoving and silent, he had watched for two days, awaiting the moment.

His shirt, jerkin, breeches and thigh-high leather boots were black. The clothes matched the cast of his eyes and the colour of his hair, hanging waist-length in a plaited ponytail. He went against custom in not wearing a beard.

A sword jutted from the ground beside him.

The wind seemed a little less fierce of late, the air a trace milder. Even here, on the slopes of Hawkstone mountain in bleak Cawdor, spring had arrived.

While the hermit looked on, the wind dropped and the leaf stilled.

He judged the time to be right. And acted with almost unbelievable swiftness.

In one fluid movement he snatched the sword with his left hand as he leapt to his feet. The razor-keen blade separated the leaf from its bough, and as it fell he sliced twice more, quartering his target. Then he plunged the sword back into its resting place before the leaf's four parts touched the ground.

A thin smile of satisfaction passed briefly across his sombre face. The year spent relearning his art had restored some of the skills.

But he knew how much better he had been when ... *complete*.

The thought, and memories of his previous life it stirred, made him melancholy again. He decided to carry out the chores he had neglected and lose himself in mindless work.

As he took up the sword and turned away, something on the plain far below caught his eye.

It was a lone rider.

From this distance he could only make out that

the stranger was coming in his direction, and that he had a spare horse in tow.

The hermit frowned. It was rare to see anyone in these parts. And he didn't welcome having his solitude disturbed. Perhaps the intruder was an enemy; someone on their way to settle an old score.

There was just one path the rider could take to reach him.

He set out to confront his unwanted visitor.

It was late in the day and the shadows were lengthening. But the hermit knew the foothills of Hawkstone well and moved slyly.

He hid in a thicket beside the solitary track.

At the sound of snapping twigs he drew his knife and crouched low. A bulky figure was climbing the path, but the bushes were too dense for his features to be seen. One of the horses he led almost slipped on the gravely surface and whinnied. The hermit saw his chance. He sprang from his hiding place.

And froze.

"So *this* is how you welcome a guest is it? *Shame,* boy!"

The hermit gaped in astonishment. "*Golcar?*" he whispered. "Is it really you?"

The older man thumped his barrel chest with a massive hand. "Aye," he grinned. "And glad to set eyes on you again!"

The young man sheathed his dagger, then stepped forward and extended his hand in greeting. In time-honoured warrior fashion they clasped flesh, the palm of each around the other's wrist.

But some of the joy went from Golcar Quixwood's weather-beaten face when he saw Dalveen Leandor's empty right sleeve.

"You seem ... fit, Dalveen," the old soldier told him. He took in their barren surroundings and added, "For a recluse."

"Life here suits me well enough. And you, Golcar, look as hearty as when I last saw you."

It was the truth. The year elapsed had hardly changed Quixwood. Perhaps his full beard was a mite greyer, and his back might have taken on a slight stoop, though his build remained robust and muscular. Overall he still appeared as tough as the sturdy cavalry boots he wore.

Except that his eyes held a world-weariness that hadn't been there before.

"But how did you find me?" Leandor went on. "And why?"

"I followed a hint here, a rumour there. Most pointed to this accursed region. As to *why*, lad..." His manner darkened. "I think you must have guessed at the grave tidings I bring."

"Tell me."

"He's back!"

* * *

The firelight made grotesque shapes on the cave's walls.

Quixwood shrugged off his dusty guard's tunic and removed his leather gauntlets. Propped against a saddle, he reached into his travel pouch for an earthenware jug of wine with a large cork stopper. He placed it on the slate floor and continued his story.

"It doesn't take a fortune-teller to know Avoch-Dar wouldn't give up. But we never expected him to return so *soon*."

Leandor lifted his gaze from the flames. "You had no warning?"

"None. They appeared at the border in the space of a single night. He has an army as great as ever, and his magic is, if anything, stronger. We couldn't hold them. They swept into Delgarvo before we mustered our defences."

"You're not a man to leave the realm in its hour of need. Why are you here?"

"On Eldrick's orders."

"How is the King?"

"Stretched to his limits and near exhausted. Yet he set about organizing resistance with a zeal that would do credit to one half his years."

"And what of ... Bethan?" Leandor asked hesitantly.

"There's bad news on that score. The wizard's

agents have seized her as hostage against her father's surrender."

"What?"

Quixwood laid a hand on his arm. "Steady, son. To the best of our knowledge she hasn't been harmed. But you must see how important it is that you come back. Now!"

"Golcar, I –"

"The King himself asks it of you! And what of the Princess's fate?"

The young warrior indicated his limp sleeve with a curt nod. "Things must be desperate if you need help from a cripple. And a coward, at that."

"No!" Quixwood flared angrily. "I won't let you speak this way! You may be many things, Dalveen, but cowardly isn't one of them."

"No doubt it's what people think."

"When did Nightshade care what people think? Or said, or did?"

Leandor permitted himself an arid smile. "It seems an age since anyone called me that."

"You can't deny it has a certain power."

"Yes. A warrior's name goes before him. It's served me well."

"Exactly! So let it go before you again. Let the name of Delgarvo's greatest champion bring hope to our friends and fear to our enemies. Return with me, and fight!"

"And how much hope or fear will people see in

a man lacking his sword arm?"

"If I know you, there's plenty of strength in the limb you have left." Quixwood sighed. "Look, Dalveen, granted you weren't our general in the first war against Avoch-Dar. But you *were* our inspiration. There was no better fighting unit than the Sabretooth Corps, because *you* led them."

"Yes. Led them so well that not one survived."

"You have nothing to blame yourself for."

"Haven't I?"

"No, damn you! They were warriors, professional soldiers like me and you. They knew the risks they were taking. And there wasn't one of them unwilling to lay down his life for his king, and for Dalgarvo. And for you."

"You always did make everything seem so simple, Golcar."

"Well, isn't it?"

Leandor got to his feet and walked to the cave's entrance. It was raining now, and he couldn't see the stars for cloud. The fire reflected off the blade strapped across his back.

"Dalveen," Quixwood said, his voice softer, "I know that Avoch-Dar's revenge on you was worse than mere death. The shame, the injury to your pride, were more punishing than the most horrible of deaths. And I think you know by now that it *was* your overweaning pride, that cocksure confidence of yours, that brought you down."

"That's one lesson I've learned this past year, if nothing else."

"Good. But don't go to the other extreme. I didn't bring you from the steps of that temple as a babe, nor teach you all I know of the martial arts, to have you spend the rest of your days brooding on a gods-forsaken mountain."

"No, please, don't spare my feelings." The tone was sarcastic.

"I'm just a bluff old soldier. I say it as I see it. And what I see here is a youth wallowing in self-pity."

"That's not fair! I –"

"If you don't like the description, boy, too bad. And if you want to make something of it, well, I could tan your hide when you were a sprout and I'm willing to try again!"

Dalveen Leandor laughed. It was something he hadn't done for a long time.

"How I've missed you, Golcar."

"And I you. But enough of this. I've brought you a horse, and there's gold coin for our journey. What's your answer?"

"I'll give it tomorrow."

"But speed is essential! While we gossip here, Avoch-Dar's horde could be massing at the gates of Allderhaven itself! And Princess Bethan –"

"I know," Leandor told him grimly. "Nevertheless it's late and the weather looks bad. We couldn't set out tonight. Now hold your peace and get some rest."

"In this hovel?" Quixwood grumbled, drawing a horse blanket over himself. Then he brightened and reached for the wine jug. "Like some?"

He gripped the cork between his teeth and grunted with the effort of easing it free.

Leandor's left hand shot to the hilt of the sword sticking out above his right shoulder. The blade cut the air in a stinging arc. It cleaved through the neck of the jug, leaving Quixwood with the cork and a chunk of neatly severed pottery sticking out of his mouth.

His jaw sagged and the stopper fell away.

"Thank you, no," the young warrior replied, smoothly replacing the weapon. "But you go ahead."

Quixwood glanced at the decapitated wine jug in his hand. "See, lad! You're as good as ever!"

"No, Golcar, not as good. But with luck, good enough to stay alive for a while."

"That may not be as easy as you think," someone said behind them.

Leandor spun around, the sword back in his hand.

Whatever he expected to see, it wasn't the figure standing at the cave's entrance.

CHAPTER 2

She was short, the top of her head barely level with Leandor's chest, and her tiny frame was stooped. Her face was wizened. Pure white, stringy hair fell to the shoulders of the drab rags she wore.

Dalveen could not tell her age, except that she was old. Very old. And she was soaked through by the rain.

"Greetings, Dalveen Leandor." Her voice was hoarse with age. "I've waited many years for this moment."

He put down his sword. "You are Melva, the wise woman?"

She nodded.

"Come in and warm yourself," he invited, standing aside to let her by.

"You know her?" Quixwood said as she slowly made her way to the fire.

"I've seen her once or twice, but we've never spoken. She has her home higher up the mountain."

"I am thought of as a hermit." The old woman smiled as she eased herself on to one of the rickety stalls at the fireside.

Leandor took a log from a pile in the corner and placed it on the flames. The wood crackled, giving out a sweet, aromatic perfume. He seated himself opposite her. Golcar perched on the crude bed of straw-filled sacking.

They regarded their guest in the light from the fire and a single candle on a makeshift table.

"How is it that you know who I am?" Leandor asked.

"I know many things, Nightshade. That is my gift. And my curse."

"It is your gift that brought you here?"

"The Fates brought me, have no doubt on that score. I was destined to come. As you were destined to find your way to Hawkstone."

"How so?"

"It is written. As it was foretold that should you ignore what I have to say, you will certainly fail in your coming task."

"You speak in riddles," Quixwood grunted.

"Then let me make myself plain. Your heart tells you to return to Allderhaven, Nightshade, and confront the evil there. Yet it would be an error to do so now."

"Would you have me neglect my duty?"

"No. You are right in believing that your place is with the King. But not yet."

"I do not see how delay would aid the cause," Golcar complained.

"We are all pawns in a greater game," Melva said. "My part in the drama is small; yours is more important than you realize, Nightshade." She lowered her head and began to cough, a hand to her mouth. Her frail body shook.

"Are you all right?" Leandor said.

"My age and the climate here exact their toll." She took a wheezing breath and continued. "I say again that you did not come to Hawkstone by chance. Why do you think you were drawn to *this* mount and no other?"

"For ... solitude."

"To lick your wounds like an injured beast, yes. And to learn a lesson in humility. You needed both. But there was another reason, though you didn't know it. I was born with but one purpose, and now that you have come at last, it will be served."

Golcar was mystified. "What purpose?"

"To relate a prophecy passed down, from mother to daughter, for a thousand, thousand generations. The burden my ancestors were forced to carry as penalty for offending the gods. A prophecy concerning you, Dalveen Leandor."

"Do I understand you to mean this ancient prediction was meant for *me*? That's beyond belief."

"Nevertheless it is so. But you must judge for yourself. Heed me, for I will not repeat what follows."

He leaned closer. "Go on."

"The prophecy is in two parts. It begins by foretelling the rise of a dreadful tyrant. His cruelty and ambition are boundless. He sweeps aside all opposition, and punishes most severely any who stand in his way. Yet he is no ordinary conqueror. For he commands a magic so terrible as to be beyond imagining."

"*Avoch-Dar!*" Golcar hissed.

"Aye. Evil is ever watchful for a human through whom it can work. In Avoch-Dar it has found such a man. His wizardry grows in strength with each passing day. Soon it will be powerful enough to rip asunder the barrier separating our world from the realm of nightmares."

"And then?" Leandor said.

"The prediction speaks of an endless reign of blood and burning. Dark will snuff out the light. Loathsome creatures from the outer regions will be let in to enslave and feed upon humanity. The future is death, Nightshade. Death and damnation."

No one spoke for a moment. The only sound was of rain pounding outside the cave.

Golcar broke the silence. "You said the prophecy has two parts."

"Yes. But the second part is incomplete. Despite the best efforts of my ancestors, a mere fragment has survived the centuries. What remains, however, offers some hope." Her shoulders heaved as the hacking cough returned.

Leandor took a wooden goblet from the table and passed it to her. She sipped from it.

Gently, he said, "Take your time."

A weak smile came to her lips. "Time is a luxury I cannot afford." Handing back the goblet, she went on. "The remainder of the prophecy, what we have of it, states that a hero shall rise to combat the tyrant. This long-awaited warrior is all that Avoch-Dar is not; courageous, noble, just. He is the only chance humankind has of salvation." She looked to Leandor's empty sleeve, adding, "And we shall know him for a dreadful loss inflicted by the power of evil."

"You seem intent on casting *me* as this mythical hero. But what proof is there?"

"The proof of my senses. I have the talent of farsight. The gods gave it to me that I might recognize you."

Leandor tried to hide the doubt he felt. "Is there more?"

"Oh, yes. The events that took place just before your birth, for instance. Are you aware of them?"

"Only vaguely. Golcar has mentioned that there were unusual happenings in the weeks leading to my discovery."

"I never set much store by them myself," the old warrior stated. "And I can't see what they could have had to do with Dalveen."

"The gods move in mysterious ways," Melva replied.

"Tell me what occurred," Leandor said.

"In the twenty-third year of King Eldrick's reign, when you were born, strange portents troubled Delgarvo," she recounted. "Rivers ceased to flow and wells ran dry. The harvest was laid waste by a plague of white ants, each the size of a man's palm. Showers of living fish fell with the rain. A statue of the goddess Thyra was heard to utter dire warnings. Dragons soared high above the monarch's palace, and a comet transformed night to day for almost a week. These and other omens marked your coming into the world."

"When did they end?"

"The night Princess Bethan was born and Queen Nerissa died. The night that Quixwood here was leading a patrol and stopped short at the entrance of a temple dedicated to the twin deities

Yorath and Eleazor. There he found you upon the steps, fresh born and bundled in coarsely-woven cloth. The same night Eldrick summoned various mystics to interpret these events, and made the mistake of welcoming Avoch-Dar into the royal household."

"I don't know what to make of all this," Leandor admitted. "Is there more to the prophecy?"

"A little. It says that to confront his foe, the warrior must regain what has been lost. That is all. We do not know what prediction, if any, was made about the conflict's outcome. But be sure that this world's fate hangs by a thread, and that Avoch-Dar's conquest of Delgarvo heralds the beginning of the end."

"Yet you advise me not to return there."

"I tell you not to return *in your present state*. Go against the sorcerer without magic of your own, and in want of your natural sword arm, and he will surely defeat you."

"As to my arm, what choice do I have?" He regarded his vacant sleeve bitterly. "The limb is gone. There is no undoing that. But do you know of sorcery to equal his?"

"Aye, the sorcery of demons." She smiled feebly. "I see from your expressions that you consider the demon time a myth. But they were real. They were masters of this world long before humans arrived."

"I will take your word on that, Melva, though I thought such tales were made up to frighten children," Leandor confessed. "What I don't understand is how a vanished race can be of help."

The old woman coughed into her palm and closed her eyes for a second. "Some of their knowledge remains. It is to be found in the Book of Shadows."

"What's that?" Golcar asked.

"A grimoire, a compendium of spells, a volume of demon lore containing undreamed of power."

"Where is this book?" Dalveen said.

"To the east. In the place that lies beyond the furthest shores of the Opal Sea."

An icy chill coursed through his veins. "Zenobia," he whispered.

"Yes, Zenobia. The land of darkness. Isle of tears and bitter sorrows. It was the hub of the demon empire."

"No one goes to that accursed region!" Quixwood exclaimed.

"A few have, in search of the book and other treasures. None returned."

"Why should I fare any better?" Leandor said.

"Perhaps you won't. The prophecies offer no guarantee of success. But one of the legends surrounding the Book of Shadows says it can be found only by the right person, and that he shall be pure of heart. Anyone wanting to use its power for evil invites disaster."

Her face looked deathly pale. And her eyes, their lids drooping, carried more weariness than Leandor had noticed when she arrived.

"I'm sorry, Melva, if coming here has tired you. If you wish to rest, we could make you comfortable and –"

"No." With an obvious effort, she smiled. "It is life that tires me. But as I told you, I have lived as long as I have to reach this moment. There will soon be time enough for me to rest. Time enough and more." The sadness in her voice was plain.

Leandor considered insisting that she rest, but he could see that her will was strong. He put another question instead. "By all accounts, Zenobia is at least as big as Delgarvo. How would I go about finding this book?"

"That is simple. From landfall, travel eastward. Eventually you will come to the book's hiding place. You must also learn to trust your instinct. That will help you in your search. If you live that long."

A flurry of sparks rose from the fire.

"For this would be a journey fraught with more than ordinary dangers," she continued. "Be warned that many perils lie in wait for any who quest after the book, some laid as traps by the demon race."

"What are these perils?" Golcar demanded.

"No one knows. But the legends say each is lethal. Make no mistake, Dalveen; every step you take will be dogged by hazard."

"You talk of predictions and destiny. So what difference would it make if I simply forgot all you've said? If our path to the future is already marked out –"

"You overlook free will. Through wrong decision a man may undo all that the gods intended." The racking cough cut through her and she paused to gather breath. "Go to … Allderhaven … and you court … certain … death." Her voice had begun to falter. *"Death … for … all."*

She swayed, and her head rolled to one side. Leandor leapt forward and caught her before she fell.

Golcar got to his feet. "Bring her over here, boy."

Kicking the stall aside, Dalveen carried her pathetically light body to the humble bed. Wetting his fingers in the goblet, he dabbed a little water on her lips.

"Melva," he said softly. "Can you hear me?"

She focused on him. Reaching out, she clasped his hand. *"My … part … is done."*

"Be still. You must save your strength."

"Zenobia… The … book. Promise … you … will … look for … the book."

"Melva, I –"

"Promise ... me, Dalveen ... Leandor."

He squeezed her hand tenderly and said, "I give you my word."

A smile came and her features relaxed.

Then her eyes closed for the last time.

The rain had stopped.

It was getting light by the time they gathered enough stones for her burial mound. Having laid her to rest, wrapped in Dalveen's cloak, Golcar spoke a few words from the funeral service used by warriors.

As her soul was offered to the gods, Leandor pondered Melva's words, and the promise he had made her.

High above, the clouds parted briefly, allowing sight of the mountain's snow-dusted peak. Aeons of relentless wind had carved the summit into the likeness of a bird of prey's majestic head, a gigantic effigy that gave Hawkstone its name.

Bathed in shafts of crimson by the rising sun, it seemed made of gold.

Chapter 3

Golcar Quixwood did not speak until it was time to go their separate ways.

They had ridden in silence for two hours. Now, with Hawkstone's misty peak far behind them, the trail divided. Quixwood glanced along the left-hand fork that led to Delgarvo and said, "It's not too late to change your mind, Dalveen."

Leandor reined in his black mare to the right-hand track. "No, Golcar. I'm taking the coastal road."

"Why persist in this madness?" snapped the older man, releasing the anger he felt.

"Because I must."

"But *Zenobia,* of all places, when you're needed

in Allderhaven! Dammit, boy, you're heading east when you should be going west!"

"I would ride to the gates of Hades itself if it helped defeat the sorcerer."

"I know you gave Melva your word, and her dying like that was a tragedy, I grant you. But when all's said and done, you're undertaking this quest on the say-so of an ancient crone and her half-baked predictions! The fabled book she spoke of may not even exist!"

"There was truth in what she said. I *know* it."

"Don't go chasing dreams, lad. Why make things harder than they already are?"

"Anything worth having has to be striven for. You told me that often enough yourself. Besides, as you said, I gave Melva my word. I'll join you as soon as I can."

"And how long will that be? The King has need of you *now*. Look, Dalveen, Eldrick never ordered you found when you went missing because he respected your wish for seclusion. Nor is he ordering you back now, despite the threat from Avoch-Dar. But don't you think you owe it to him, and to Bethan, to –"

"I need no reminding of my responsibility to the King," Leandor bridled, "or to the Princess. Not even from you." He looked up at the sun, then spoke in softer tone. "I must make haste if I'm to reach Saltwood by tomorrow."

"*That* den of cut-throats! You'll be lucky to find a captain there willing to take you to your accursed destination."

Leander patted the leather pouch on his belt. "I have ample coin, thanks to you, and there are always men who will risk themselves for gain."

"I should know better than to argue with you," Quixwood sighed. "At least heed my warning. The moment we part company, danger threatens you. You may have forgotten, stuck up there on your mountain, but there's a war going on down here. Take care."

Leandor smiled. "I will. Fare thee well, Golcar."

"And you, lad. I'll count the days to your return." He spurred his horse and took the Delgarvo road.

Leandor watched until the man he thought of as his father was lost to sight. Then he urged his own steed along the other track.

By midday, distance had swallowed Hawkstone.

He kept to a steady gallop and did not stop to rest. His only refreshment came from a canteen of pure mountain water, and he used it sparingly.

There was no sign of life anywhere in the wasteland he crossed until late afternoon. Then he saw, far off, a ragged line of people walking on foot. They were moving south-east, away from him, and their paths would not cross. He supposed them to be refugees, fleeing the chaos wrought by Avoch-Dar's army in the west. Later, as the sun began to set, he spotted a large party of riders, churning dust in their wake, but they were too distant to be of concern. Which was just as well, as he could not make out the uniforms they wore.

Night fell, and Leandor sought a place to bed down. He found it in a hollow formed by an outcrop of rock. Having tethered the horse, he crawled into the crevice and wrapped himself in a blanket against the chill. He made sure his sword was to hand.

His mind was alive with thoughts of the expedition he had embarked upon. And of the Book of Shadows. But eventually he drifted into sleep under the starry sky.

Dawn's first light woke him.

He breakfasted hastily on a chunk of black bread and a little of the water. Determined to lose no time, he saddled up and set off right away.

After an hour he noticed a dense column of smoke on the western horizon, and what could have been the black forms of circling vultures above. A burning village, perhaps, unfortunate enough to find itself in the way of the invading forces.

He thought of Golcar and hoped his journey home held no unpleasant surprises.

The landscape started to change. It was less

rugged, with clumps of coarse green weeds beginning to appear. As he pushed on, the barren earth gave way to a carpet of grass, and the trees increased. When they thickened to a wood he dismounted and led his horse into it.

In the depths of the timberland he came across a mature ganva bush. Cutting free one of its ripe, purple-green fruits, he sliced away the peel. The pulpy interior looked appetizing, but he had to spit out the bite he took. It tasted of salt.

At least it confirmed he was near his goal.

He walked on. The ground sloped upwards and the trees thinned. He topped a ridge and found himself on a hilltop looking down at Saltwood.

The sprawling town that had grown around the port seemed unplanned. Its crooked streets were lined haphazardly with unmatched buildings of varying height. Chalky white cliffs framed either side of the harbour. Between them, scores of ships bobbed at anchor on the Opal Sea, a vast expanse of clear water that stretched endlessly ahead.

He felt as though he had arrived at the edge of the world.

After a year alone, the sights, sounds and smells of the place almost overwhelmed him.

The narrow cobbled lanes were crowded with peoples of many nations, and a constant chatter of unfamiliar tongues came from all sides.

Leading his horse through the press of bodies, he was jostled by beggars, swaggering drunks, street entertainers and ragged urchins. Merchants guided mules through the mob, laden with bolts of coloured fabric and sacks of pungent herbs. Costermongers, strolling musicians and fortune-tellers bellowed their wares. Sickly clouds of incense drifted from the open doors of temples.

He passed a row of stalls piled high with fruit, vegetables, cheeses, bread, sweetmeats and infinite varieties of fish. A pack of mangy dogs ran around the legs of the food sellers. Nearby, a squealing pig nosed discarded titbits in the rubbish-strewn gutter. Clucking hens fluttered to avoid the careless feet of passers-by.

Leandor needed a base, somewhere to stay while he searched for a ship to take him to Zenobia; and his horse should be watered and fed. He decided to make his way to the docks. Elbowing through the crowd, he found a turning that led down to the harbour.

He was relieved at how much quieter it was once he left the main streets. But his instinct told him the warren of passages he entered was less safe. Unsavoury characters lounged in doorways. Hard-faced men whispered to each other in shadowy corners.

A noisy group of seamen reeled from a tavern. Several of them stared with open curiosity at his black garb and empty sleeve. He readied himself for trouble. But they staggered off, arms around their companions' shoulders, a slurred song on their lips.

At length he came to an inn with stables. A weather-beaten sign swinging above the door identified it as *The Wayfarer's Rest*. He tied his horse to the hitching rail and entered.

It was dingy inside. The air smelt of old ale and stale pipe tobacco. A handful of drinkers, most of them sailors, quietened and turned sullen eyes in his direction. He ignored them and crossed to the rough-hewn counter. The landlord, a brawny man, his head shaved, nodded curtly.

"I seek lodgings," Leandor said.

"Two silver pieces a night. In advance." He studied the vacant sleeve.

Leandor dug into his money pouch, aware of the men watching him. "I want to eat, and my horse needs stabling."

"That'll be three silver pieces then."

The innkeeper took the coins and bit each in turn with yellowed teeth to be sure they were genuine. Satisfied, he dropped them into an apron pocket, then jerked his thumb at the staircase beside him. "Upstairs, first door. I'll bring the food."

Soft conversations resumed as Leandor climbed the creaking steps.

The room was plainly furnished. But it was clean, and there was a decent fire in the hearth. He drew the only chair to the window and surveyed the view. In the harbour, ships' masts rocked gently against the blushing sunset. Leandor wondered which vessel would carry him to Zenobia, assuming he could persuade anyone to undertake the hazardous voyage.

His thoughts were interrupted when the landlord arrived with a tray. He placed it on a small table and left without a word. The bowl of spiced stew and seeded loaf still warm from the oven were surprisingly good. They went well with the flagon of honey-laced ale.

After eating he returned to the tavern's drinking room. There were many more customers now and he felt less conspicuous. As he moved through them it became obvious that the main topic of conversation was Avoch-Dar's assault on Allderhaven. But although there was much gossip and rumour, there were few hard facts.

He spent an hour or so asking after a ship on which to book passage, loosening tongues with rounds of drinks. The name he heard most often was Captain Seth Hartern. Having learned the berth at which Hartern's ship, *Windrunner*, was anchored, Leandor decided to go there. He slipped quietly into the cool night.

The main passageways were lit by pitch torches

set in metal brackets on the front of every third or fourth house. But few of the alleys branching off on either side had any lighting at all.

As he passed one of these, someone ran out of the darkness and collided with him.

He stepped back, ready to draw his blade.

The guttering flame of a nearby torch gave just enough light to make out the stranger's features.

At first, he thought it was a boy. Then he realized that the panting figure was a young woman, a year or two less than his own age, and not quite as tall as him. Her blonde hair was cut short like a man's and encircled by a red sweat-band. Under her green waistcoat she wore a white cotton shirt with flowing sleeves. Her black breeches were tucked into tan boots. She looked fit and lithe.

And she was holding a knife.

She eyed him warily. He guessed she could not decide whether he was friend or foe. Yet she stood with a defiant stance.

"What's wrong?" He spoke mildly, to reassure her.

"Nothing."

"Can I help?"

"No." Her eyes darted to the alley she had come from and her body tensed. "Just let me pass. I'm in a hurry."

"I can see that. Why?"

"It's personal." Her expression hardened. "Now move!"

"But—"

"You heard her," a gruff voice interrupted. "It's *personal.*"

They spun to face the alley. A man had emerged from its black maw. Bare-chested except for a sleeveless leather jerkin, he had on the baggy pantaloons and studded ankle-boots favoured by street brigands. There was a curved scimitar in his hand.

The woman hissed, *"Damnation!"* and raised her knife.

"This is no business of yours, one-arm," the bandit told Leandor. A gold tooth glinted in the pearly whiteness of his self-important smile. "On your way!"

"I prefer to stay," Leandor said evenly.

The brigand threw back his head and let out a scornful laugh. "Hear that, boys?"

Three similarly dressed men slid out of the shadows. Their blades were drawn. They joined the first man in a menacing semicircle before Leandor and the woman.

"He prefers to stay!" the leader mocked. "Big words from a cripple, eh lads?"

"A porpoise short of a flipper!" one of them shouted, and they roared with laughter.

"He'll be short of both when we've finished

with him," promised the leader. "And his purse!"

Leander glanced at the girl. He thought her expression showed more determination than fear. He looked back at the leader and said coolly, "I'm ready whenever you are."

"I think you lack a brain as well as an arm," the man retorted, provoking further glee from the others.

"And *I* think you and your fellow scum are tired of living, serpent breath."

The grins vanished from the bandits' faces. They moved forward.

Leandor reached for his sword.

Chapter 4

The sword was in his hand before the bandit leader advanced two paces.

On Leandor's left, a man edged toward him with weapon raised. To his right, the girl drew back as the brigand nearest her moved in. The fourth man kept to the rear, gazing at Leandor's face.

In that moment, Dalveen realized he had forgotten how the prospect of combat felt.

Forgotten the rush of energy that surged through his veins. Forgotten the heightened sense of reality that set his nerve-endings tingling. Forgotten the way confronting death intensified life.

Now the feeling returned. It was exhilarating, and frightening. It was like being born again.

Then the brigand on the left yelled, "He's mine!" and rushed in.

Leandor didn't bother to look at him. He flashed his sword outward and upward. The tip went in above the man's belt buckle, travelled rapidly up his chest and left at the chin. He collapsed, lifeless.

The blade carried on in an overarm arc and struck the oncoming chief's scimitar with a resounding crash.

Simultaneously, the girl leapt aside, narrowly avoiding a slicing swipe from her attacker.

Features twisted with rage, the leader charged, brandishing his sword two-handed. Leandor parried every slash with practised ease, adding frustration to the man's fury. The sound of steel on steel echoed in the deserted lane.

Dodging a savage thrust, Leandor half turned and caught sight of the girl. He was just in time to see her hand shoot out and fling the small knife. It struck her opponent square in the chest. He looked down with amazement at the protruding hilt, swayed, and fell. She reached inside her sleeve for another blade.

The leader kept up his battering onslaught. Leandor was nimbler, swifter and more experienced. But the brigand chief's murderous anger made him unpredictable. And a man whose actions could not be predicted was dangerous. A duel with any of the finest swordsmen in Delgarvo would not have given Leandor concern. Facing the worst would.

It was time to end this.

He renewed his attack, pushing forward without let up. The leader began moving back and his swordplay became a series of wild defensive strokes. Stumbling on the uneven cobbled surface, he dropped his guard. Leandor prepared to exploit the opening.

There was a blur of movement on the edge of his vision.

He vaulted to one side, spun, and saw the fourth man coming at him with sword held high. The leader quickly regained his footing and prepared to lunge. Leandor's reckoning was thrown off-balance by the new threat and he hesitated for a split second.

The charging brigand stopped dead in his tracks. He gave a gasp, staggered a pace and went down. One of the girl's knives jutted between his shoulder blades.

Leandor swiftly returned his attention to the stunned leader. He took a sweeping slash at him. The man blocked it with the edge of his scimitar, but the bone-jarring impact rocked him back on his heels. As his sword reached the limit of its swing, Leandor wrist-flipped it around and brought it straight down again. Another crashing blow, and the leader retreated further.

Hacking left to right, right to left, striking the scimitar with each pass, Leandor drove onward. The constant rain of stinging metal forced the bandit across the lane's width. Then his back was against the opposite wall and there was no escape.

In a frenzy of desperation he launched himself outward, seeking a way through the thrashing storm that trapped him. Leandor side-stepped the whistling scimitar. Then he dropped to a half-crouch and met the returning weapon with his own. The collision hurled the bandit back to the wall and knocked his sword arm aside, leaving his upper body unprotected. Leandor threw himself forward.

And plunged his blade into the brigand's heart.

The man's face was a picture of stupefied surprise. He gave a low, rasping grunt. His eyes rolled until only the whites showed.

Stepping back, Leandor tugged at his sword. It came away with a wet swish.

A shudder ran through the man and life departed. His body slowly slipped to the ground.

Leandor looked for the girl. She was kneeling by one of the dead men, wiping her knives on his jerkin.

"Come on!" he called. "There may be more of them."

"There are," came the curt reply. "Just a minute." She tossed back her copious sleeves to reveal leather scabbards tied to both arms. Each held a row of the snub-bladed throwing knives, and she quickly replaced the two that had been used. Then she got to her feet and said, "Let's go!"

Side by side, they made off at speed toward the harbour. There was nobody else on the streets.

A few minutes later, with the docks in view and other people about, they slowed to walking pace. After looking back to be sure no one was following them, Leandor thanked her for killing the brigand. She just nodded.

When she did speak, she asked, "How are you known?"

"My chosen name is Dalveen Leandor."

"Truly? The one called Nightshade, the King's Champion?"

"I ... once held that position."

"I believe you," she decided, "though you are widely thought to be dead. Slain a year past, by..." She seemed to have trouble finishing.

"By Avoch-Dar," he offered.

"Yes. Avoch-Dar. The foulest of the foul."

There was bitterness in her voice, and not a little sorrow. He judged this the wrong time to enquire why. Instead, he said, "I'm not so easy to kill. But the sorcerer left me a legacy." He glanced at his pinned sleeve, and her eyes followed. "You haven't told me who you are," he added.

"I'm Shani Vanya. And I suppose I should thank you for coming to my aid. But I could have handled those rogues myself."

"I don't doubt it," he smiled. "Who were they?"

"Members of the Guild of Thieves."

"How did you incur *their* wrath?"

"Oh, a trifling dispute over a hoard of gems they say I took."

"Do you have them?"

"Not any longer."

They laughed, and their moods lightened.

"Is it your habit to make such powerful enemies, Shani?"

"I try not to. And they're hardly going to be too pleased with you either, come to think of it." She looked about the dockside. "Where to now?"

"I don't know about *you,* but I was going to see if I could book passage on a ship."

"Your tone makes plain you don't crave companionship. Neither do I. But I'm looking for a ship, too."

Leandor felt slightly ashamed. After all, this woman may well have saved his life. "Where are you going?" he said.

"I don't mind, as long as it's away from here."

"The Guild, eh?"

"Yes. They're particularly strong in Saltwood.

Just along the coast would do me fine. But I've had no luck finding anyone to take me."

"Maybe the skipper I've been told about can help."

"I appreciate it, Dalveen. Where are you heading?"

"Zenobia."

She started to laugh, then stopped when she saw he was serious. "You're not joking, are you? Why in the name of the gods go *there*?"

"To ... find something."

"Good luck, then. But almost anywhere else will suit me, thank you very much."

Avoch-Dar watched Dalveen Leandor and the young woman as they strode toward Saltwood harbour.

He had seen and heard enough for now. With a wave of his hand their image vanished from the spy crystal. It was replaced by a swirl of vivid colours on the surface of the huge gem. The sorcerer continued staring at the shimmering display, idly stroking his beard with talon-like thumb and forefinger.

On the other side of the war tent, eleven of his generals stood to attention in nervous silence.

At last the wizard turned to them, his long, bony face intense. All avoided meeting the gaze of his disturbing eyes.

"It seems Nightshade has lost few of his skills, despite his crippled state." He chuckled low and sinister.

The comment was addressed at no one in particular, and the generals knew better than to respond without permission.

Their master snapped his fingers. A servant came forward bearing a cloak of dark velvet with a silver pentagram embroidered on its back. He placed it about the magician's shoulders and, bowing low, scurried away.

"And now the reason you are here," Avoch-Dar announced coldly. "Bring in the prisoner!"

The tent flaps pulled aside and three figures entered. Two were zombie guards, pathetic shambling creatures enslaved by the sorcerer's magical will. Gaunt, skeletal brutes with black-rimmed, lifeless eyes, their taut yellowing skin barely covered their skulls. Hideously fixed grins stretched wide their lips, exposing rotted, broken teeth.

Their captive was middle-aged, with white hair and moustache, and wore a uniform identical to the other commanders present. His face was etched with terror.

The undead minions forced him to kneel before the wizard.

Avoch-Dar greeted the cowering man in mock good humour. "Welcome, General Trantez. How kind of you to come."

Then his expression changed to simmering fury as he looked to the assembled warlords. "Your colleague, gentlemen, the twelfth of your number, has seen fit to disobey me."

The man kept his gaze fixed to the floor and quailed.

"His orders were to take the western approach and clear it of defenders. A simple enough task. Yet he failed."

"But my lord," Trantez pleaded, "they fought with such spirit that we –"

"Do not whine to me about the Delgarvian rabble's spirit! *What spirit did* you *show in crushing them?"*

"My lord, I –"

"Silence, cur!"

The generals exchanged tense glances.

"I shall not be defied!" Avoch-Dar bellowed. "Nor will I tolerate any interference with my plans!"

He raised his hands and began to weave a spell.

Trantez cringed with fear as the wizard towered over him. "No, master!" he begged. "Please! Have mercy!"

"The only mercy I show cowards," the conjuror raged, pointing down at him, "is death!"

A shaft of dazzling fire flashed from Avoch-Dar's fingertips and engulfed the general.

He contorted in pain, his mouth forming a soundless scream.

Then the surging light surrounding him grew so fierce that only Avoch-Dar's eyes could endure its blinding intensity.

Suddenly it ceased.

The spot where General Trantez knelt was hidden by acrid smoke. As it dissolved, to muffled coughs from several of the warlords, the victim's fate was laid bare.

The man who lived and breathed only seconds before had gone. All that remained was a pool of viscous crimson liquid. It seethed vilely against the richly-patterned rugs. Bubbles erupted on its surface and gave out a foul odour as they burst.

Avoch-Dar smiled.

"Look well upon this," he told his generals. "The same fate awaits any who fall short of what is demanded of them."

He stared hard at each grey, frightened face in turn, then swept out of the tent.

They stumbled in his wake, still blinking, and glanced appalled at the remains of their comrade as they passed.

Five hundred bonfires and twenty times that number of burning brands lit the inky darkness. Countless thousands of men, and things that walked like men, made ready for the final assault on Allderhaven.

The capital's walls stood stark on the horizon.

Beyond, the towers of the royal fortress, Torpoint, could be faintly seen.

Chapter 5

"I think this should be enough." Captain Seth Hartern weighed the pouch of gold in his hand and smiled.

"That's fortunate," Leandor replied dryly, "as it's all we have."

"Most skippers wouldn't accept ten times this amount to brave the destination you're bound for."

They stood with Shani at *Windrunner*'s rail, looking out at the twinkling lights of Saltwood. "What will your men make of a voyage to Zenobia?" she asked.

Further along the deck, several of the crew huddled together, whispering and looking their way.

The Captain's full-bearded, weather-beaten face took on a harder cast. "They'll do as I tell 'em." He hefted the pouch, clinking the coins. "And spreading a few of these around will calm their doubts."

"When do we sail?" Leandor said.

"With the midnight tide. Be on board with your mounts in good time. But remember, under no circumstances will I put ashore at Zenobia. We'll anchor off the coast and ferry you over by boat."

Leandor nodded.

"All right. Now I have cargo to load." Hartern moved off, barking orders at the deckhands.

On their way down the gangplank, Leandor told Shani he was returning to the inn for his horse.

"I don't have one, Dalveen, but I'll sort that out now and see you here before twelve."

"Perhaps we should go together. If you run into any more Guild members –"

"Then I'll deal with them. No offence, but I prefer to be alone. I'm used to it."

He shrugged, then laid his hand against *Windrunner*'s sleek hull. "We seem to have found a trim vessel at any rate. It should make good time."

"Zenobia's hardly a place I'd be anxious to rush to," she laughed. "What do you feel about Hartern? Can he be trusted?"

"Who knows? But he's been paid well enough for his services."

"Yes, in advance. Who's to say he won't drop us over the side and save himself the trouble? It might be best to sleep with one eye open."

"You mean you don't anyway?"

When they met again, Shani was leading a pure white gelding.

"Handsome horse," Leandor observed. "And all the more remarkable a purchase considering Captain Hartern took the last of your coin."

"I didn't *buy* it exactly," Shani admitted. "More borrowed it, you might say. And you can wipe that look of disapproval off your face! It didn't come from anyone who couldn't bear the loss."

"Wouldn't it have been better to wait until you reached your destination?"

"Use your common sense, Dalveen! You always *borrow* a horse in the place you're about to *leave*."

He smiled. "I'll remember that."

Windrunner was abuzz with last minute preparations for sailing. They got a passing crewman to direct them to an area at the stern where livestock was corralled. Once they had secured the horses, another man explained the way to their cabins.

After a couple of wrong turns below deck, they found the door to Leandor's quarters. Shani opened it and went in first.

There was a man inside with his back to them.

He spun around, a sword in his hand.

She instantly produced a knife and flung it at him. The deftly-aimed missile pinned the sleeve of his sword arm to the wall. He dropped his rapier.

Leandor, his own weapon drawn, swiftly kicked the sword away. Then he brought his blade point up to the intruder's chest.

"Steady, friend, steady," the man said. His voice was calm, and he held Leandor's eyes in an even gaze.

"Who are you?" Shani demanded.

"Just another passenger."

"What are you doing in my cabin?" Leandor underlined the question with a none too gentle jab.

"*Your* cabin? I thought it was mine. Forgive me. A genuine mistake, I assure you."

Like Dalveen, the man was clean-shaven, but his fiery red hair flowed loose to his shoulders. He wore light, short-sleeved chain-mail over a brown shirt, and studded leather wrist protectors. His heavy wool breeches and stout boots, along with his muscular build, marked him out as a professional warrior.

"Why the sword?" Shani asked.

"I saw a rat. Filthy creatures. Can't abide them."

"You still haven't said who you are," Leandor reminded him.

"I'll be glad to tell you anything you want to

know." He glanced at his skewered sleeve. "But is there need for this?"

Leandor and Shani looked at each other and swapped nods. She went over and removed her knife.

"Any sudden move," Leandor warned him, "will be your last. Now sit on the bunk. Slowly. And let's have some answers."

"My name is Craigo Meath," the stranger said as he perched himself.

"You're obviously military. Which master do you serve?"

"None. I'm a freelance."

"A *mercenary*." Shani made it sound like a swear word.

"I prefer to be called an independent soldier," Meath said indignantly.

"I'll bet you do," she sneered.

Leandor intervened. "Where are you bound?"

"Along the coast, to Delgarvo Peninsula."

"Why?"

"To reach Allderhaven the quicker, and stand with King Eldrick against Avoch-Dar's army."

"Think again, Meath. The King doesn't employ mercenaries."

"I do not go as one. My decision to back Eldrick has nothing to do with money."

"What, then?"

"Even a soldier of fortune may pledge himself

to a cause. And defeating the sorcerer is as good a cause as any I know. It would be a bleak future indeed with Avoch-Dar as our ruler."

"Not to mention bad for business in your line of work."

"I don't deny it. Avoch-Dar has need of slaves, not free fighters like me. Should he win, my kind faces extinction." He flicked aside a rust-coloured lock of hair. "Talk to Captain Hartern if you doubt my story."

Shani moved away. "That's exactly what I'm about to do. If he tries anything, give him a taste of steel, Dalveen." She left, slamming the door.

Meath grinned, displaying a set of strong, white teeth. "Spirited, isn't she? But at least she confirmed my suspicion. You're Nightshade, aren't you?"

Leandor did not respond.

"It was obvious before she used your name, man. The missing arm, the black garb..."

"The man you speak of is widely assumed to be dead, surely?"

"Well, I never believed it. I always favoured those stories that said he survived his last encounter with the sorcerer. You *are* Nightshade, aren't you?"

"And if I am?"

"Then I'm honoured to meet you. Your exploits

are an inspiration to fighting men everywhere. You are widely admired among my trade's brotherhood. Even those you've beaten speak your name with respect."

"Really? I don't remember leaving alive any of the mercenaries I've met in combat."

"Lost your arm but not your sense of humour, I see." Meath smiled.

Leandor didn't.

"And now you're on your way back to Delgarvo," the mercenary continued, "to help fight the invader."

"No, not Delgarvo."

Meath was surprised. "But surely..."

The door opened and Shani came in.

"The Captain confirmed that he's booked passage," she told Leandor. "And we're about to get under way."

Leandor gave Meath his sword back. "Time for you to find the right cabin."

"Thank you." He sheathed the weapon. "Perhaps we'll have a chance to talk properly later."

"Perhaps."

Meath walked to the end of the corridor and turned the corner.

"I don't like him," Shani decided.

"I don't think you like *anybody*."

"That's not true. It's just that he's a little too sure of himself. A bit arrogant, I suppose."

"Well, we only have to put up with it for a day or two, then we'll all be going our separate ways."

"True."

An hour later they stood on deck and watched the distant lights of Saltwood fade into darkness.

Shani was curious about Leandor's background. He told her of his youth in Allderhaven, and the kindness King Eldrick and Golcar Quixwood had shown him. She was a good listener, and his instinct was to trust her.

Then he said, "Now tell me about yourself. How did you become such an accomplished knife-thrower, for instance?"

"I've been alone for a long time. At least, it feels that way. I had to learn to look after myself or go under. Knife-throwing seemed an obvious choice, so when the need arose I practised every day. I'm useful with a sword, too, and a reasonable archer. But the knives are best. They let you avoid close-quarter fighting, and make you the equal of any man. It's a case of coping with the situation you find yourself in." She nodded toward his vacant sleeve. "I think you understand."

"Yes. When Avoch-Dar destroyed my arm I had to learn how to fight all over again. As you say, it was that or go under."

Leandor noticed how, as before, a pained expression had come to Shani's face when the sorcerer was mentioned. "What is it about the wizard that troubles you so?" he asked. "Something does, or your feelings wouldn't be so obvious."

It seemed she wasn't going to answer. But after a moment, her gaze fixed upon the dark, choppy waters, she began to speak.

"I was born near a village close to the Vaynor border. My family were farmers. It was hard scraping a living so close to the edge of the desert, but we managed. And we were happy. When Avoch-Dar marched his army into Delgarvo for the first invasion, we thought ourselves lucky when they passed us by. It was the week of my fifteenth birthday, and I remember watching that great mass of soldiers moving along below the horizon.

"What we didn't know was that they were sending out raiding parties from the army's flanks. The next night, one of them reached our village." She paused, and her eyes misted.

"Shani, you don't have to –"

"No, it's all right." She cleared her throat and carried on. "My father sent me to hide in the fields. There were only a couple of dozen men in the raiding party, but they were hardened warriors. The people in my village were farmers, herdsmen and traders. No match for soldiers. Avoch-Dar's men put everyone to the sword."

"Your family?"

"All slain. My mother, father, brothers, uncles, aunts, cousins... Not content with that, the soldiers slaughtered the livestock and poisoned the wells. And what they couldn't carry away they burnt."

"But you escaped."

"Only by pure chance. I hid in a cornfield the whole night, too frightened to move. Once, I thought I was trapped by the fires they'd started, but the wind changed and sent the flames in another direction. When I crawled out at dawn, the soldiers had gone."

"What did you do then?"

"There was nothing left for me in the village. Hell, there *was* no village any more. So I took to wandering, and I've been looking for my place in the world ever since." She turned and gave him a weak smile. "I haven't found it yet."

"I'm truly sorry," he said gently. But he knew there were no words to soothe her troubled heart.

They stood silently together for some time. Then, although he hadn't meant to tell her, he related his meeting with Melva, the wise woman, and explained why he sought the Book of Shadows. He thought it might give her some hope.

When he finished, she said, "I confess it crossed my mind that you might be running away. I feel ashamed about that now."

"Don't. You're not the first to think it of me."

She stretched and yawned. "It's been a long day. I'm going to turn in."

"Of course."

"Oh, there was something I forgot to tell you. The Captain said he's going to take you to Zenobia first, before dropping me along the coast. And Meath, of course."

"That seems a strange route. Surely where you're going is nearer?"

"Yes, but he said it has to do with tides or currents or something. I suspect it's to get it over with and settle the crew. The idea of Zenobia isn't proving too popular with them."

"That doesn't surprise me."

They said goodnight and retired to their cabins.

Leandor lay awake for a long time, his mind churning with thoughts of what Shani had told him. He dwelt too upon the King, Bethan and Avoch-Dar.

And far into the sleepless night he wondered what the first peril might be.

Chapter 6

The speeding knife flashed in the spring sunshine and thudded into the mast.

Another embedded itself next to it. Then four more followed in blinding succession. The half-dozen blades formed a glinting circle on the wooden column.

Shani drew back her arm and lobbed the seventh. It struck home in the centre of the metal ring.

Applause and ragged cheers broke out.

She turned to the waiting sailor and said, "Your turn."

He didn't have proper throwing knives like Shani's. His heavy belt held a row of daggers, slender and staccato sharp. Each had curled handguards where the hilt met the blade.

The crewman aimed below her display. His first throw was true. The second landed slightly out of alignment, but near enough to make the curve of a circle. Blades three, four, five and six quickly completed the loop. He concentrated hard before tossing the seventh at the bull's-eye. It cleaved the air.

Then hit the mast awkwardly and spiralled off to bury itself in the deck.

Laughter and hoots of derision came from his shipmates.

"My game, I think." Shani held out a palm. With good humour, but red-faced, he slapped several pieces of silver into her hand.

A bell rang to mark the change of the watch. The crew members who had gathered for the contest drifted away to their duties. Shani went to retrieve her knives.

Leandor strolled over. "Don't you *ever* lose?"

"If I did, I wouldn't be able to pay the bets."

Meath joined them. "Bravo! With talent like that you should think of taking up my line of work, girl."

"I am *not* a girl!" she flared. "I'm a woman. And I wouldn't be a mercenary for all the gold in Eldrick's treasury."

Not for the first time, Meath thought her outburst amusing. "Temper, temper," he chided.

Leandor noted Shani's sour expression. Three

days on board *Windrunner* hadn't improved her opinion of the man. But what really seemed to irritate her was that he never took her insults seriously.

"I have news," the grinning mercenary told them. "The Captain says we should be in sight of Zenobia any time now. Which will at least ease the boredom of being stuck on this leaky bucket for so long." He gave Leandor an accusing glance. "Although why *anyone* would want to go to that –"

"Yes, Meath, we've heard it all before," Shani snapped, turning her back on him. "How about some sparring, Dalveen?"

He shrugged. "All right."

"And I'll fight the winner!" Meath called as they walked away.

Shani snatched a cutlass from a nearby rack and gave a few practice swipes. Leandor drew his sword and they squared off.

Meath stayed for ten minutes before losing interest and wandering away.

Shani attacked Leandor's blade furiously, putting all her strength behind each blow. "Hey!" he cried. "This is only practice, remember?"

"Sorry." She stepped back, lowering the weapon. "It's that damned Meath," she fumed. "He makes me so *angry*, I could..."

"It won't be for much longer. He'll be gone soon."

"And so will you," she said glumly. "I'll miss you, Dalveen, and I'll be thinking of you."

"Thanks, Shani. Who knows? Perhaps one day we'll—"

"Land ahoy!"

The lookout in the crow's-nest was pointing to the starboard horizon. Far distant, where sky touched sea, a black line was just visible.

Captain Hartern came along the deck. He noticed their quizzical looks. "Aye," he confirmed, "that's Zenobia."

"When will we reach it?" Leandor asked.

"We're making good headway, so we'll be there this evening. But you won't be put ashore till dawn. The waters off that coast are treacherous. I'll not risk it by night."

"Whatever you say, skipper." Leandor returned his sword to the scabbard on his back.

"And, er, there's one more thing I might not have the chance to tell you later," Hartern added. "Your identity isn't exactly a secret on board. You haven't told me why you're so anxious to reach that gods-forsaken port of call yonder, and that's your business. But I'll wager it has something to do with Avoch-Dar. We seafarers have suffered at that devil's hands, too, and I reckon it'll be the worse for all of us should he come out on top. If you're looking to do him some harm, then good luck to you."

It was the longest speech they'd heard him make, and Leandor was grateful for it. "Thank you, Captain. I'll do my best."

The skipper nodded and left.

They watched Zenobia's shoreline draw closer.

By late afternoon they were near enough to make out the haunted isle's brooding cliffs.

The atmosphere aboard *Windrunner* changed. An air of tension could be felt. The crew muttered to each other in hushed tones as they eyed the approaching land mass.

Their mood was made no better by gathering storm clouds.

Captain Hartern did his best to keep the men busy, but they went about their chores with ill grace. More than once Leandor and Shani were aware of reproachful glances.

Evening brought rain and wind. The ship bobbed in swelling waves. All hands set to trimming the sails and securing deck cargo.

An hour later the rain was pounding down relentlessly. *Windrunner* rolled as breakers hit. A man was assigned to help the helmsman control the wheel.

The Captain ordered the vessel anchored a safe distance from shore to ride it out. He also suggested, with as much tact as he could, that his crew would work better without passengers in the way.

Shani, Meath and Leandor took the hint. They abandoned a frugal supper and went to their cabins.

As the night wore on, the storm grew heavier. *Windrunner* rocked violently.

Leandor, stretched wide awake on his bunk, listened to the tortured creak of wood and rigging. On the other side of the hull, inches from his head, waves crashed. Muffled shouts and thuds came from above.

He thought he heard a scream. Or was it the howling wind?

Then the door exploded open.

Shani stood there, soaked to the skin, holding a cutlass.

"*Quick!*" she panted. "Something's happening!"

"They can handle the storm, Shani."

"No, it's not *that*! Come on!"

He grabbed his sword and rushed up the stairs.

A full-blown gale lashed the ship. The decks were awash. Thunder boomed and lightning ripped across the sky. It showed a picture of confusion. Men were running in all directions. Some tugged at lines. Others wrestled with a half-collapsed sail.

But it wasn't just the storm they fought.

Toward the stern, a large, indistinct shape loomed over two crewmen. Leandor couldn't make out what it was through the pummelling rain and flying spray.

"What's going on?" he bellowed.

"I don't know! Something ... something *strange*!"

Another flash of lightning. One of the sailors wielded a sword. The shape bore down on them. Darkness returned and a scream rang out.

"Get a lamp!" Leandor shouted. Shani ducked back into the stairwell.

He looked up to the quarterdeck, shielding his eyes from the rain. There was no one at the helm. The wheel spun free.

A loud crack sounded behind him. He turned and saw a bulky silhouette on the other side of the rail. It flowed over the wooden barrier and on to the deck.

Blinking in the downpour, he retreated a step as the thing advanced.

Then Shani was beside him with a lantern. She held it high, bathing the scene in light.

They faced a creature unlike anything either of them had seen before.

It was big, half as tall again as a man, and shaped like an elongated pyramid. The slimy green hide, rippling constantly, had the look of wet leather. Instead of legs, it moved on a skirt of writhing tentacles, similar to an octopus. But there were arms. Stubby and muscular, they ended in webbed paws with razor-keen talons. There was no neck between its body and domed head.

The face was a nightmare. Its eyes were yellow slits with jet black orbs at their centre. Twin gills pulsated below. All else was gaping mouth.

"My gods!" Shani cried. "What *is* it?"

"Hostile!" Leandor took a swipe at it with his sword. The blade scythed through the monstrosity's torso. But it left no wound in its wake. Jelly-like flesh absorbed the blow, ebbing back to reform itself instantly.

The creature opened wide its huge maw and displayed wickedly sharp fangs. A hissing gurgle rose deep in its throat. It inched forward.

Leandor struck at it again and again, to no effect. Shani darted out and plunged her cutlass into its side. The only result was an overpowering fishy stench.

It was nearer now, and its arms were raised. One of them slashed downward. Leandor grasped Shani's jerkin, pulling her aside. The monster's claw raked the wall where they'd been standing and gouged slithers of wood.

Leandor and Shani ran for the prow. They had an advantage in being able to move faster than the pursuing creature. But the deck was pitching giddily and it was hard to keep balance.

They reached a corner just as another of the amphibious beasts came around it. Skidding to a halt, they saw it had a struggling crewman in its arms. The screaming man's kicking legs were clear of the deck. He was trying to hack at the creature with a cutlass.

Shani thrust her own sword through her belt and whipped out a knife. She flung it with all her might. It impacted in the monster's upper body and was swallowed by spongy flesh. Leandor was aware of the first horror closing in behind them as she fumbled for a second blade.

"Aim for the head!" he roared.

This time her knife struck the creature's right eye. It gave a throaty roar and dropped its captive. He rolled away and tried to stand. His feet scrabbled on the slippery deck.

Suddenly another man appeared. In a flash of lightning, Shani recognized him as the sailor she won the money from earlier. He had a dagger in each hand. Rushing at the monster from behind, he drove them into its back. The other man, upright now, charged in and began slashing the enraged brute with his cutlass.

Leandor urged Shani past them. Ten paces further along they saw a creature dragging a dead or unconscious crewman to the rail. Before they could do anything, it crashed through. Monster and man disappeared over the side.

They pushed on. Bodies of sailors littered the deck. Beyond, at the prow, three figures fought a pair of the abominations. When they got nearer they realized that two of the group were Meath and the Captain. The third was a deckhand. He and Meath were laying about a creature with their swords. Captain Hartern was fending off the other with a barbed harpoon.

Leandor pitched in with a massive two-handed swing at the creature menacing the Captain. The blade severed its arm. Hartern lunged forward with a powerful thrust that sent the harpoon clean through the beast. It collapsed twitching to the deck.

The man fighting alongside Meath was caught by the second creature's slashing claw and went down. Then the monster turned on Leandor. It moved with unexpected speed and he almost lost his footing as the gleaming talons sought his face.

Suddenly, Meath was between them, holding off the beast with his sword. Leandor quickly regained his balance and added his blade to Shani's and the mercenary's. They forced the creature to the rail and it went overboard.

"Thank you!" Dalveen mouthed over the gale. Meath acknowledged with a wave of his sword.

There was an explosive snapping noise. The deck lurched crazily.

"The anchor's gone!" Hartern yelled. "*Abandon ship!*"

Buffeted by mountainous waves, *Windrunner* swept toward the Zenobian shore.

"Follow me!" the Captain shouted. "There's a boat amidships!"

They saw no living crewmen as they dashed after him. But more shadowy forms were swarming aboard behind them.

Hartern got to the boat first and began untying its restraining ropes. When they caught up with him, he cried, "You do this! I'm going to cut loose the livestock and give them a chance!"

"I'll come with you!" Meath offered. "We'll be back!" he told the others.

The Captain and the mercenary headed for the stern and vanished from sight.

Leandor set to slashing the ropes with his sword. Shani held the lamp for him.

Something touched her shoulder.

She spun around. A hissing creature loomed over her, no more than a sword's length away. She brought up her cutlass. And had it knocked out of her hand by a blow from a scaly claw.

Springing forward, Leandor's blade cut into the creature's back. But his dive took him too close. A tremendous blow smashed him to the deck.

The creature turned and lurched in Shani's direction. Her cutlass was lost somewhere in the darkness. She needed a knife but there was no time to free one.

In desperation, she flung the lantern at the monster.

It shattered against its chest and the oil instantly detonated. The creature was engulfed by flames. It moaned terribly. Blazing the entire length of its body, it staggered away, moving jerkily toward the bow. A trail of fire marked its progress along the deck. When it blundered against the rail, and then the forward mast, the oil ignited them too.

Dragging her eyes away from the shrieking fireball, she went to Leandor. He was on hands and knees, shaking his head to clear it. She helped him up.

The ship gave a stomach-jolting heave.

Shani looked outward to the ocean. They were being driven straight toward jagged black rocks.

She clutched his arm and screamed, *"Dalveen!"*

Then chaos and darkness took them.

Chapter 7

Something rough scoured his cheek.

Leandor opened his eyes. It was daylight. His horse, soaking and bedraggled, lent over him, licking his face. He gently pushed her away.

He was on his back, staring at a clear sky. The previous night's storm was spent. His body ached and his head was sore, but no bones seemed to be broken. Slowly, he sat up.

A beach stretched out in front and behind him. Its pebbly sand was black. Just to his left, mild waves lapped the seashore, and the ocean beyond was calm. Much further to his right, ominous cliffs formed an endless barrier in both directions.

Weak sunshine reflected on an object half

buried in the sand. Leandor reached out stiffly and found it was his sword. He must have hung on to it, despite the tempest. Handling the familiar weapon made him feel a little better, and he slid it into its scabbard as he got to his feet.

He went to the steed and made a fuss of her, rubbing her damp mane and whispering soothing words in her ear. Then he scanned the beach, confirming that he was alone. The thought came that Shani, Hartern, Meath and the others had probably drowned because of him, and he felt a flush of guilt.

His brooding came to an end when the mare whinnied and tried to pull toward the water's edge. He followed her gaze and saw something emerging from the sea.

Perhaps it was one of the infernal creatures that invaded the ship. He hoped it was a survivor, carried to Zenobia's shore by the tides, as he had been.

When it proved to be neither, relief mingled with disappointment.

It was another horse, a grey colt he'd seen tethered on *Windrunner*'s deck, although he didn't know who it belonged to. The animal shook itself, spraying droplets, then approached him shyly. He patted its snout.

Leandor decided to move on. Ahead, distant cliffs jutted far into the sea, making an impassable headland. There was no such obstruction to his rear, where the beach snaked round the wall of rock and was lost from sight. He led the horses that way.

His boots squelched moistly. As the sun grew stronger, his wringing wet clothes and the horses' coats began to steam. He kept a constant watch on the ocean. Nothing else, living or dead, came out of it.

But when he finally rounded the bend and discovered a cove, he saw two people walking in his direction.

They were Shani and Meath.

Shani ran forward and threw her arms around him. "Dalveen! Thank the gods you're safe!"

Meath caught up and offered his hand in warrior's greeting. "Well met, Leandor," he grinned. "I see you even managed to rescue my horse!"

"He's yours?"

The mercenary nodded and took his mount's rein. "Aye, and we've come through many a campaign together." He ran a hand along the colt's flank. "I'd thought I'd lost him."

"I confess I thought I'd lost *you* two," Leandor admitted. "Are you all right?"

"Nothing serious," Shani told him, "just cuts and bruises. But my horse washed up dead, I'm afraid. I lost a couple of my knives, too, which is irritating."

"You're lucky you didn't lose your life," Meath said, more serious now.

She glared at him. "Yes. Fate has been kind to us."

"Has it?" Meath persisted. "This is Zenobia, remember. It might have been better had we perished at sea."

Leandor could do without them bickering again. "Have you seen anyone else from *Windrunner*?" he asked.

They shook their heads. Shani pointed to the sea's edge. "Just that."

Several pieces of wreckage had washed ashore, mostly smashed wood and tangled ropes.

"What happened after you and Hartern left us, Meath?" Leandor said.

"We got to the livestock and managed to release them. Then more of those damned monsters attacked us. The Captain was dragged over the side by one, poor devil. I was about to suffer the same myself when we hit the rocks. The next thing I knew was coming round here on the beach with Shani standing over me."

She shuddered. "What *were* those things?"

"I don't know," Leandor replied. "Well, not exactly." He carried on before they could question that. "Look, it seems you two have no choice but to accompany me. Unless you want to stay here on the chance of another ship passing, which is extremely unlikely." He glanced at the sea. "The tide will be coming in soon. Shani's been told something of what I'm up to, Meath. I suggest we find somewhere a bit more hospitable and I'll explain the rest."

Meath pointed to the curve at the bay's other end. "Around there we noticed a crevice that might lead to the plateau above. It's a steep climb, but I think we can do it."

As they set off, Shani said, "Have you noticed anything, Dalveen?"

"What?"

"There's no birdsong."

She was right. Apart from the crashing waves, all was silent.

The roar of battle filled the air.

Screams of men and wounded horses combined with clashing steel in a constant background din. A shower of arrows, numbering thousands, rained death on the struggling mass.

Avoch-Dar took no notice.

Seated on a hill overlooking the field of conflict, he gave his attention to the magic crystal standing on a rostrum before him. It showed Leandor, Shani and Meath crossing the beach, the horses in tow.

A silent group of warlords, slaves and servants awaited their wizard master's pleasure, ready to serve his slightest whim.

He sank back in his jewel-encrusted throne, his gaze still upon the crystal. "So, Nightshade has reached Zenobia," he muttered, "despite opposition from the depth-dwellers. And it seems his party has grown."

No one spoke. No one dared.

There was a commotion at his side. The ranks of attendants parted and a messenger rushed through. He hurled himself to the ground at the sorcerer's feet, eyes cast low. "If it pleases my lord," he intoned with trembling voice.

"Hmmm?"

"Tidings from the southern front, my lord."

Avoch-Dar sighed and turned his fearsome eyes on the grovelling lackey. "Speak."

"Resistance is fierce in that sector and our losses are heavy. General Wykom respectfully requests reinforcements, lord."

"Must I always be bothered with such trivia?" snapped the wizard. The man winced. "Tell Wykom the only message I wish to receive from him is one announcing his successful breach of the city's defences."

He dismissed the messenger with a contemptuous wave of his hand.

Bursts of intense light erupted against Allderhaven's walls as favoured minions used magic against them.

The battle raged on.

Avoch-Dar returned to the crystal.

* * *

It was mid-morning before they got themselves and the horses to the top of the cliffs.

A vast expanse of land spread out in front of them. There were no trees, just scrubby grass and weeds as far as they could see. Dismal clouds hid the peaks of remote mountains. The eerie silence remained unbroken.

They sorted the few possessions they'd managed to retain and laid out some of their clothes to dry. Apart from a handful of hard ship's biscuits that had somehow survived intact in Shani's pocket, there was no food. But there were two canteens of water, which would have to be rationed. The horses grazed as best they could on the meagre plant life.

Meath had his sword. And something as vital to them as their weapons: several flints wrapped in waterproof resin, which meant they could make fire. Although they had to be used as sparingly as the water.

As the trio settled to rest, Leandor gave the promised explanation. Meath listened attentively as the tale of Melva and the Book of Shadows unfolded. Like everyone else, he knew the legends of the demon time, but had never heard of the book.

When Leandor finished, Meath said, "If you're on a mission that might bring down Avoch-Dar, I want to be part of it."

"Me, too," resolved Shani.

"There's something I haven't told either of you yet," Leandor added. "This quest is fraught with particular dangers."

"I guessed *that,*" Dalveen," Shani replied.

"No, I said *particular* dangers. Obstacles quite apart from the usual hazards we might expect. Or should I say unusual, bearing in mind the grim reputation this place has? The demons left *specific* perils for anyone seeking the book."

"What are they?" she asked.

"Melva couldn't say. But those creatures must have been the first."

"You mean we're going to face *more* of that kind of thing?"

"I don't know what we're going to face, except that all the perils are deadly. We'll have to keep our wits about us. The prophecy comes with no guarantee of success, remember."

"I'm just a soldier, plain and simple," Meath said, "and talk of prophecies I take with a pinch of salt. They have a way of getting muddled with the passage of time. But magic's real enough, we all know that. So let's find the book. There's one thing nobody's mentioned, though. Assuming we're successful, how do you suggest we get back to Delgarvo? Swim?"

Leandor shrugged. "We'll worry about that at the time. If we live long enough."

"I'm not sure this is wise," Leandor said.

Meath dumped a stack of branches, then huffed into his cupped hands. "The temperature's still dropping, man. It's either a fire or we freeze, and if we don't get ourselves dried properly we invite fever."

They'd ridden eastward all day, Leandor sharing his horse with Shani, under a sun too feeble to draw out the dampness in their clothes. But the vegetation became more abundant the farther they travelled. As night fell, moonless and chill, they came to a vast forest. Rather than enter it in the dark, they made camp.

Shani appeared with another bundle of wood.

"I think this should be enough." She jerked her thumb in the direction of the tree line. "And I'm sure I heard water flowing over there."

Leandor nodded. "Me, too. We'll have a look later. But we'll do it together. I don't want anyone wandering off on their own in the dark."

Meath knelt, took out two flints and rubbed them together briskly until orange sparks flew. Soon, the trio was gathered around a blazing fire.

"Let's not get so enchanted by the warmth that we forget where we are," Leandor cautioned.

"No fear of that," Meath said, unsheathing his sword. He drove it into the ground and sat next to it. "I intend being ready for anything."

Shani squatted opposite, next to Leandor. "You haven't said much for the last couple of hours, Dalveen. Why so gloomy?"

"I suppose I'm troubled by the loss of Captain Hartern and his crew. They'd still be alive if I hadn't made them bring me here."

"You didn't *make* them. The Captain took gold in exchange for the risk. He knew what he was doing."

"That does little to ease the guilt, Shani."

"You must have felt the same way about the Sabretooth Corps," Meath commented.

Leandor's face hardened and he made no reply.

"Why do I know that name?" Shani wondered.

Meath took Leandor's silence as an invitation to

explain. "They were an elite cavalry unit our friend here captained. Every one of them was wiped out in the last battle against Avoch-Dar the first time he invaded. Isn't that so, Leandor?"

"Yes." The answer came reluctantly, and he kept his gaze directed at the flames.

"I've often wondered how that came about," Meath added. "What happened, exactly?"

Shani glared at him. She could see it was a painful subject for Leandor.

He lifted his eyes from the blaze and looked at the mercenary. "There's no mystery. I led them in a charge against the wizard's bodyguard. None lived to tell of it. Many would call it a reckless action. And, yes, I regret their deaths."

"They were professional soldiers, Dalveen," Shani said kindly. "No blame can be attached to you."

"You're not the first person to tell me that recently," he replied, remembering his conversation with Quixwood. "But an officer has to take some responsibility for the welfare of his men."

"The girl's right," Meath declared, ignoring Shani's offended expression. "When you live the life of a warrior you have to accept that some of your comrades will fall. It's a fact of war. If you survive yourself, you lift a glass in their memory. Otherwise it's best to put them out of mind."

"You weren't at the battle yourself, then?"

Leandor said. "Despite your support of the King."

"Well, no. But not from want of trying. I was coming back from the Amrac Islands and tangled with a gang of pirate scum. You know how they infest those waters. By the time I got to Delgarvo it was all over."

"I see."

Shani reached for a canteen. One swallow drained it. "How about going to fill this now, Dalveen?" she suggested.

"All right. Keep your eyes open, Meath."

They made for the trees. In their shadow, they stopped and listened to the running water.

"That way." Shani pointed deeper into the forest. As they walked toward the sound, she whispered, "I still think Meath's arrogant."

"Had we met a year ago, you may well have thought the same of me."

"I find that hard to believe."

"A twelve-month of solitude changed me. I looked to my flaws, and worked to right them. So I can't condemn a man for something I've been guilty of myself. And he's lent his sword to our cause so far. Not to mention coming to my aid against that monster on board the ship."

"True. But he was tactless to dwell on the Sabretooth Corps' fate when it obviously troubles you so."

"Perhaps. Many fighting men become hardened to the realities of death and can appear callous. All I'd say to you, Shani, is that this mission is perilous enough without us arguing amongst ourselves. We need to work as a team, and watch each others' backs."

"I understand. You want me to go easier on Meath. I'll try."

The ground began to slope and the noise of running water was close. They scrambled down the incline, careful of their footing in the darkness, and found a rushing stream.

Shani got on her knees, dipped her hand in and shivered. "It's like ice!" She sucked her fingers. "Tastes all right though."

"It would be safer if we could work out a way of boiling it."

"Can't see how, with nothing to boil it in." She filled the canteen and got up. "We'll just have to..."

A twig cracked loudly.

Something moved in the shadows to their right. Then stopped.

They stood motionless, straining to hear. Half a minute slowly crawled past before the stillness was broken again, this time by a swish of leaves underfoot. Whatever was out there was coming closer.

Leandor quietly drew his sword. Shani carefully

placed the canteen's strap over her shoulder. She slipped a knife from her sleeve.

The rustling grew noisier. And they knew now it was being made by more than one pair of feet. They crept up the slope. Shani looked back, but saw only darkness. Leandor spurred her in the direction of their camp with a wave of his sword. He kept to the rear, head turned to catch a glimpse of whoever stalked them. Still nothing could be seen.

They increased their pace. The unseen pursuers did the same. There was no longer a pretence of stealth. Branches snapped. Bushes could be heard whipping aside as bodies brushed against them.

Shani and Leandor began to jog. The sounds behind grew louder. Ignoring the danger of falling in the dark, the pair started to run. The retreat had become a chase. More than once they had to dodge tree trunks that loomed unexpectedly in their path.

The commotion came after them, crashing through the undergrowth in the wake of their headlong flight. But the hunters remained hidden. It was all Leandor and Shani could do to stay ahead of them.

Finally they reached the end of the forest. They could see the light of their campfire on the plain beyond, Meath silhouetted by the glow. Lungs bursting, they dashed in his direction.

"Meath! *Meath!*" Leandor yelled.

The mercenary looked over, then leapt to his feet, sword in hand. He met them a few steps from the fire.

"What's wrong?"

"Something ... somebody ... coming after ... us," panted Shani.

"Who? What?" Meath demanded, scanning the shadows.

"Couldn't see," explained Leandor. "But it sounded like quite a number. Be ready!"

They faced the trees, weapons raised.

Nothing happened at first. Then there was movement at the timberland's edge. Figures became visible, although the gloom and distance made them indistinct. As they slowly approached it was possible to see that there were at least thirty of them. They looked human, but much shorter than an average man or woman.

"I don't like the odds," Leandor said. He glanced at the horses, hitched to a log some way beyond the fire. "Our best chance is a hasty retreat. Agreed?"

Shani and Meath nodded.

"Come on, then!"

As they started for the horses a great war cry went up.

The figures charged.

They moved fast, covering the stretch of open

ground with astonishing speed. In seconds the leading runners had got to the fire.

"We're not going to make it!" Meath shouted.

Leandor swung around to confront the attackers. "Brace yourselves! And show no quarter!"

Two figures dashed at him. They were small. Not tiny like dwarfs, but about the height of a child of ten or eleven; the tops of their heads perhaps level with Shani's chin. And they were much brawnier than any normal youngster. They were armed with hatchets, clubs and knives. As they closed in, Leandor had the impression that their faces and bare chests were decorated in some way.

He stopped the first with a low body-slash. The second caught a stinging whack to the side of his head from the flat of Leandor's blade and went down.

Meath was confronted by three opponents, one brandishing a spear. He knocked the weapon aside and plunged his rapier into the man's chest. Then he slashed at another's face. The blow sent the assailant shrieking headlong into the fire. He rolled from the flames and lay still. The third kept out of range, warily eyeing Meath's flashing sword.

Shani dealt with two of the foe in quick succession. She saw off one with a knife throw to his ribs; the other took a blade in the thigh.

But more of the enemy were swarming from the trees and joining the fight.

The trio backed away, swinging wildly with swords and knives to keep them at bay.

"It's hopeless!" Shani exclaimed. "There's too many!"

"Then we'll go down fighting!" Leandor told her, hacking his blade into a man's shoulder.

Another cry, a single voice this time, came from the direction of the trees. It must have been a signal, because the men they fought suddenly fell back.

"What now?" Meath wondered.

His answer came in the form of a high-pitched whistling in the air above. Scores of arrows struck the ground in front of them. A line of men clutching short curved bows rushed forward with fresh shafts loaded on taut strings. They took up a firing position.

One of the archers jerked his head at Leandor, Shani and Meath in turn. It was obviously an order to drop their weapons.

They hesitated. Instantly another volley of arrows hit home just short of their feet.

"We've no choice," Leandor decided. "We can't fight bows with blades."

Reluctantly, he let go of his sword. Meath did the same. Shani tossed away the knife she was holding.

Their captors moved in and seized them. Probing hands snatched Leandor and Meath's daggers. Shani's knife holsters were ripped from her arms.

As they were manhandled, they got their first close look at the warriors. All were small, but muscular, and sported long, flowing black hair. Several had head-dresses of white feathers. They wore brown or green loincloths, and leather moccasins.

The most startling thing about them was their skin decoration. Vividly coloured loops, circles and jagged lines covered their faces, arms, legs and every other piece of exposed flesh. It was hard to tell whether the patterns had been painted or were tattoos. The skin itself appeared to have a blue-green tinge, but that too could have been pigment.

A tribesman jabbed his spear at the captives, and barked something in a guttural, unknown language.

Leandor, Shani and Meath were marched into the dismal forest.

They were made to walk with spears and knives at their backs, while the horses were led at the rear of the party. Except for occasional whisperings in the strange, unknown language, their captors were silent.

Eventually they came to a clearing in the depths of the forest. It was lit by a bonfire, and burning brands lashed to wooden posts. The light showed about twenty roundhouses with thatched roofs. Most were quite small, but three or four looked big enough to hold scores of people.

More of the oddly decorated forest-dwellers appeared, along with several womenfolk and children.

The trio were herded to the middle of the clearing and immediately became objects of curiosity. The natives swarmed around, prodding the prisoners and chattering amongst themselves. Leandor's missing arm, Shani's cropped hair and Meath's flowing red locks fascinated them. But the mob seemed inquisitive rather than hostile.

Leandor noticed a tribesman sweep out of one of the largest huts. He was a little taller than the rest and massively built. His head-dress was much more ornate, and he carried a slender, multi-coloured spear. Half a dozen warriors walked respectfully a few paces behind.

A hush fell upon the crowd and it parted to let him through. As he approached, Leandor saw that his skin decorations were the most elaborate of all. More significantly, it was his proud posture that marked him out as a leader.

Shani obviously thought so too. "This must be their chief," she whispered.

The tribesman closely scrutinized each of the captives in turn. Then he barked an order. The trio was seized and frogmarched to one of the smaller huts.

They were roughly thrown in and the door barred.

Shani picked herself up and said, "Why haven't they killed us?"

Meath dusted his clothes with a flicking hand.

Under other circumstances the look of distaste he wore would have been comical. "We're dealing with savages. Who can tell how their primitive minds work?"

Leandor pushed against the door. "This place is built like a prison."

On the opposite wall there was a series of narrow horizontal openings to let in air and light. They weren't wide enough to get a hand into, but they could be looked through. Meath pressed his face against them and called the others over.

The view was of the central clearing and an adjoining hut. As they watched, three natives appeared. Two carried baskets laden with fruit, the other an earthenware jug, which they placed in front of the hut's door. A tribesman moved forward hesitantly and knocked. Immediately, all three ran away.

"What in Hades is *that* about?" Meath wondered.

"Supper time for the chief, perhaps?" Shani said.

Leandor was doubtful. "That wasn't the hut he came out of. I expect we'll see who it is in a moment."

They watched on and off for the next hour, but no one collected the food.

Then their own door opened. Two spearmen came in, followed by the three natives they'd seen earlier. They dumped a bowl and jug on the floor as the spear-carriers stood guard.

After they'd gone, Shani examined the offering and gave a disgusted grunt. "Stale, gritty bread and foul water. Hardly a feast."

"We're obviously considered less important than their other guest," Leandor observed.

"Who isn't hungry," Meath grumbled, turning from the slats in the wall. "The food over there is still untouched."

"Did you notice those men's teeth, Dalveen?" Shani said. "They looked really sharp and jagged."

"Yes. Perhaps this is a tribe of carnivores who've never taken to eating cooked meat. If that's the case, over time they would have developed the kind of teeth needed to deal with raw carcasses."

"Now *there's* a pleasant thought."

"As I said," Meath reminded them, "we've fallen into the hands of barbarians."

"Could be," Leandor replied. "But not so uncivilized that they've neglected to feed us, even if not very well." He glanced at the paltry meal. "Look, you two, I don't think they would have bothered feeding us if we're to be killed. Not immediately, anyway. Let's get some rest."

They tried.

But none of them slept very much that night.

When dawn came, Shani moved to the wall

openings and looked through the slats. "That food and drink still hasn't been touched. What in fury's name is going on, Dalveen?"

"I'm just as baffled as you are. But rather than waste time wondering, let's try getting out of here."

They spent the rest of the day examining their prison inch by inch. If there were any weak points, they didn't find them. So they gave up and took turns sleeping.

When darkness came again the trio watched as the ritual of the night before was repeated at the other hut. Three men laid down baskets and a jug, collected the untouched food, knocked and fled. No one came to the door.

Shortly after, a commotion outside brought Leandor, Shani and Meath back to the openings.

"It looks like the entire clan," Shani whispered. "And there's the Chief. You were right about him not being in that hut, Dalveen."

Meath said, "What are they doing?"

"I can't... Just a minute." She pointed. "Look!"

A group of natives was marching toward the crowd, driving a dozen or so prisoners ahead of them. Their frightened expressions could be plainly seen in the torchlight.

"They must be members of another tribe," Leandor remarked.

The men were of normal height and seemed to

tower over the many heads surrounding them. They wore loose-fitting white robes and rope sandals. Unlike their captors, they lacked skin decorations and were bearded.

One of them was forced to his knees in front of the Chief, two tribesmen holding fast his shoulders. The Chief raised his arms and addressed the mob in a loud, clear voice. His words had the rhythm of a chant.

"Sounds like some sort of ritual," Shani guessed. "If only we knew what he's saying!"

But no knowledge of the language was needed to understand what happened next.

The Chief finished his incantation and pointed at the prisoner. A guard grasped his hair and pulled back his head. Slowly, the Chief approached and knelt before the struggling man. The crowd held its breath.

Then they saw the knife in the head tribesman's hand.

A hideous shriek rent the air. And suddenly cut short. The Chief moved in on the lifeless captive.

Finally he got to his feet and faced the crowd. His lips and chin were plastered with shiny wetness. A great roar of approval went up from the tribe.

"It's *horrible,*" Shani gasped.

Leandor squeezed her arm to steady her. "I should have guessed. *Flesh-eaters!*"

"It's not over yet," Meath told them.

The Chief made a gesture with his hand and the tribe fell upon the other prisoners. Their dying screams were quickly snuffed out.

Leandor, Shani and Meath watched what followed with revulsion. With so many mouths to feed it was over in minutes. Then what remained of the bodies was dragged away and the tribe melted back to their huts.

"My gods," Shani muttered.

Meath looked grim. "Us now, do you think?"

"Perhaps not," Leandor told him. "Let's hope they've sated themselves for a while."

"Those fiends are keeping us alive until they need to feed again, aren't they?" Shani said.

Leandor nodded. "It looks that way. And that might be tonight. Or tomorrow at best."

"What are we going to do?"

"All we *can* do is try to overpower the guards and get our hands on their weapons."

"What good will a couple of hatchets or spears be against so many?"

"They'd give us a chance, Shani, no matter how small." He paused. "And if the worst comes to the worst ... well, we can use them on ourselves."

His companions glanced at each other, then nodded their agreement.

"All right," he continued. "Maybe they won't come tonight. But if they do, we'll..."

There was a sound outside.

They tensed, ready for a fight.

The door inched open. Behind the small burning brand it held, stood a hazy figure. It stepped in. As their eyes adjusted to the light they made out its features.

What they saw amazed them.

Avoch-Dar was furious.

He smashed down a fist on the oak table bearing his crystal. The image of the visitor at the door of Leandor's prison dissolved in swirling mist.

The wizard turned his wrath on the officer standing to attention beside him. "Why must you always bring me problems? Eldrick cannot *have fled! He must be here somewhere!* Find him!"

Saluting crisply, the subordinate dashed off along the corridor, elbowing through a stream of soldiers coming the other way.

All was noise and chaos within the walls of Torpoint, Allderhaven's royal fortress. Fighting raged on the floors above and two of the castle's towers had still to be cleared.

It was vital that the King be taken immediately. The magician could not move to the next stage of his plan without him. But his men had yet to locate his hiding place.

Now this.

He glared at the magic crystal. Nightshade's quest

had taken an unexpected turn. And Avoch-Dar did not like surprises.

Four members of his personal bodyguard were positioned nearby. "Bring me the Princess!" he snapped. "And protect this crystal well in my absence! If harm befalls it, you forfeit your lives!"

He strode off to supervise the search himself.

It was definitely not human.

As small as the vampire tribesmen, the creature was covered entirely in shaggy, reddish-brown fur. It was very muscular and gave the impression of great strength.

The hand that held the burning torch had sharp claws, but there was no sign of any on the creature's feet, or indeed any indication of toes. It was unclothed except for wrist bands and anklets, made of variously-coloured metals. A shiny strip was wrapped around its waist.

A head that seemed too big for its body topped a squat neck. The fur on its face was shorter and near golden. Its huge, round eyes were pure green, and all the more startling for having no lids. What passed for its nose was little more than two small, flat holes, although its mouth and teeth looked similar to a human's. The ears were pointed and swept back, not unlike those of a horse.

It took a step towards them.

Shani gasped. Leandor prepared to leap at it.

Meath, the nearest, rushed forward and delivered a heavy punch to the thing's chin. Then yelped with pain and retreated clutching his stinging fist. The creature showed no reaction.

Leandor propelled himself shoulder-first into the hairy barrel chest. Had his target been a normal man, the force would have downed him. But Leandor felt as though he'd charged a stone wall. He pushed as hard as he could, to no avail.

Shani came in from the side and grabbed the creature's raised arm. She pulled down with all her weight. It didn't move.

"Sirs, madam," the creature intoned in a high, piping voice, "there really is no need for violence."

Amazed, Leandor and Shani let go. "It talks," she said.

"I am perfectly capable of vocalization." The strange intruder sounded offended.

"Who ... *what* are you?"

"A homunculus, my lady. But this is not the time for explanations. We must make good our escape."

"Escape?" Leandor queried.

"Indeed, sir. If you care to accompany me I will take you to your weapons and horses."

"Don't trust it!" Meath snapped, rubbing his bruised hand. "It's a trick."

"There is no deception, I assure you." The thing regarded them with unblinking eyes.

"Just a minute," Leandor said. "Were you in that hut next door?"

"Yes, sir," the creature replied.

"And you were being held captive, like us?"

"Oh no, sir, more an honoured guest. These people think I'm a god. Or at least some of them do. The rest cannot make up their minds."

"Then why leave?"

"Being treated as a god is extremely tedious. The tribe is either worshipping me or constantly offering me food. As I have no need to eat or drink, it became very boring."

"What kind of a monster is it that neither eats nor drinks?" Meath said. "No good will come of this, Leandor."

"What have we got to lose? It seems to me that either we go with this ... person, or we wait here to be slaughtered."

"I agree," Shani told them. "But tell me... Do you have a name?"

"Tycho, madam." The creature gave a slight bow of his head.

"Tell me, Tycho, why haven't you left before now?"

"Simply because I had nowhere better to go."

"You mean you want to come with us?"

"That is all I ask in return for helping to free you, my lady."

"I'm for trying it," Leandor decided. "Meath?"

The mercenary sighed and nodded reluctantly.

"Excellent," Tycho said. "We should go now, while some darkness remains. But it would be wise to extinguish this." He dropped the torch and ground it underfoot. "Follow me."

He turned and left.

They crept after him.

All was quiet and there were no natives to be seen. Tycho led them across the clearing to one of the smaller huts, where they found their weapons. Horses were tethered outside. Leandor and Meath untied theirs while Shani selected one for herself.

"We'll walk them out and mount when we're clear of the village," Leandor whispered.

They headed for the forest.

A loud yell broke the silence.

The doors of huts flew open. Scores of heavily armed natives poured out and ran at them from all directions.

In seconds, they were surrounded.

They stood back to back, ready to face the onslaught. A multitude of spears, clubs and knives confronted them on every side.

But the tribesmen did not attack. They stood warily just beyond sword range.

"Why are they hesitating?" Leandor wondered.

"They are in a dilemma," Tycho replied. "If they kill you, they run the risk of losing a meal. And those who believe me to be a god are probably a little afraid."

"Do you have any godlike powers that might be of help?" Meath asked hopefully.

"I do have certain abilities, sir, but alas they are unsuited to this particular situation. And in any event I am incapable of harming humans."

"Marvellous!" The mercenary's tone dripped sarcasm. "A lot of good *you're* going to be!"

"There is no need to despair," Tycho assured them. "Salvation is at hand."

"Unless you can come up with an army in the next two minutes," Shani said, "I find that hard to believe."

"We have nature on our side," the odd creature stated. "You have only to hold them off for a short time."

Meath gave him a hostile look. "Very reassuring."

Leandor nodded over the heads of the encircling natives. "Here comes the Chief. Brace yourselves."

Features twisted with rage, the headman arrived beside his warriors. He raised his spear and bellowed.

The tribe moved in.

A wide, powerful swing from Leandor's blade immediately cleaved the chests of two men, sending them sprawling back into those behind. Without pause he slashed the face of another, then grounded a fourth with a swipe that laid open his thigh.

Shani hacked at the arm of a native with her knife, wrenched away his spear and turned it on him. A man with a hatchet charged her. She spun and jabbed at his ribcage.

Meath dodged under the guard of a spearman

and ran him through. A warrior taking his place succumbed to a thrust of cold steel. The next pitched over when Meath's rapier found his exposed belly.

Confronted by an opponent wielding a machete, Leandor surged in and inflicted two swift downward strokes. They carved a slicing cross in his foe's torso. Wailing, the man spiralled away.

As he swerved to avoid a swinging hatchet, Leandor caught sight of Tycho. A native was delivering a tremendous blow to the creature's head with a club. Tycho didn't seem to notice. The man with the club looked stupefied.

Leandor found himself fighting shoulder to shoulder with Shani. "We can't hold them off much longer!" she yelled.

Wave upon wave of the screaming enemy crashed against the trio's blades.

"Look to the west!" It was Tycho, and he pointed at the treetops to their right. The sky above was turning crimson.

"Dawn!" Meath cried, batting away a thrusting spear.

The great red orb of the sun began to appear.

"They are moon-worshippers, beings of the night," Tycho explained. "They *fear* daylight and believe that taking life in view of the sun god will curse them!"

The tribesmen were backing off. Several turned and dashed for the shelter of huts. As the first shafts of sunlight penetrated the gloom, panic set in. Forgetting their enemies, the warriors scattered, dropping weapons as they ran.

Rapidly, the sun rose, until half its diameter was clearly visible. The village was bathed by increasingly strong rays. Doors slammed as the natives sought sanctuary in their crude shelters.

Shani tugged at Leandor's sleeve. "Come on! Let's get out of here while we can!"

Tycho and Meath joined them in their race for the horses.

The mercenary quickly mounted and spurred his animal across the clearing, snatching a burning torch as he went. Riding to a hut, he reached over and set light to its thatch. He moved on to the next building, and the next, igniting each with the brand.

"Meath!" Leandor shouted. *"Meath!"*

The soldier of fortune ignored him and carried on spreading the fire.

"Saddle up, Shani," Leandor ordered. "Tycho, can you ride a horse?"

"I need no mount, sir. I can match your speed, and I do not tire."

Meath rode back to them, tossing away the torch. The village blazed.

"I see your mercenary ways die hard, Meath."

"It's them or us, Leandor. You know that. Now shall we leave this accursed place?"

They made for the forest, the awful shrieks of the dying ringing in their ears.

The column of smoke was far behind when they came to a river. They stopped to rest on its banks.

"Was it really necessary to torch that place, Meath?" Leandor asked. "It was obvious we could escape without further loss of life."

"Of course it was necessary. I'm surprised at such a question from a professional soldier."

"Making one's life as a fighter doesn't mean acting brutally."

"Come now, Leandor. Remember what they were going to do to *us*. I don't know about you, but I don't like the idea of being stalked by those flesh-eaters." He pointed at Tycho. "Surely it's more important that we get some answers from ... that."

"Of course I would be happy to answer any questions you may put to me," Tycho told him.

"I still don't understand what you *are*," Shani said. "You mentioned being a hom ... something..."

"A homunculus, my lady. An artificial creature, if you will. I was not born but made, and my maker fashioned me with alchemical magic."

"Who made you?"

"A wizard of great infamy, madam. You may know his name. Avoch-Dar."

"*What?*" Meath leapt to his feet and drew his sword. "I knew there was something rotten about this creature. Stand aside, Leandor, and I'll rid us of it."

"I believe you would find that rather difficult, sir," Tycho stated calmly, "unless your blade can counter the magic that sustains me. Which I doubt."

"Let's simmer down," Leandor said. He turned to the creature. "Tycho, what you've just told us comes as quite a shock."

"You can say that again," Shani put in, far from happy.

"Avoch-Dar is our mortal enemy," Leandor continued.

"Good. I obviously made the right decision in joining you."

"Must we stand here bartering words with the thing?" Meath fumed. "If Avoch-Dar made it—"

"Then why tell us that?" Leandor interrupted. "It's hardly the action of an enemy spy. And Tycho saved us from the cannibal tribe."

"Yes," Shani agreed, "he did do that. We owe him a hearing." She fixed the creature with a hard gaze. "But if we don't like what you have to say, little man, we'll *find* a way of finishing you."

"I understand your misgivings, madam. But, as I said, disposing of me is no easy task. I believe that as I was made by magic, it would take magic to slay me. I may even be immortal."

"All right," Leandor said. "Let's start at the beginning. *Why* did Avoch-Dar create you?"

"I think I was some kind of experiment, sir, a task the magician set himself to test his powers. Being the kind of man he is, he designed me as a plaything, a jester to amuse him. And to be the butt of his cruelty. For, you see, the magician deliberately made me with *feelings*, so that I would suffer the more at his hands. You must know he takes pleasure in the pain of others, and what enjoyment is there in tormenting a creature lacking emotions?"

"I know full well the delight he feels at causing torment," Leandor confirmed, eyeing his empty sleeve. "What did you mean when you said you can't harm human life?"

"Having conjured into existence a being that was practically indestructible, Avoch-Dar realized I might be a threat. Not to *him*, because his magic could overcome me, but to his followers. So he cast a spell making it impossible for me to directly or indirectly injure anyone."

"And if you tried?"

"I would experience pain, and if I persisted, my destruction."

"But in every other way, you have the same feelings as a human?"

"Yes, sir. I know happiness, joy and sadness as you do. But giving me emotions was a mistake on the wizard's part. Because they include anger, resentment, an understanding of injustice and a desire for revenge. Thus I came to hate Avoch-Dar. And not only for what he did to me. I witnessed his naked ambition and countless vile acts many times. I soon saw the danger he poses to the world."

"How did you get away from him?" Shani asked.

"As he planned to invade Delgarvo for the second time he grew more and more obsessed with the scheme. He neglected his toys, not least myself. In truth I think he was tiring of me anyway. But that made it easier to plot my escape."

"You ran away?"

"I tried, madam, and was caught. It would have been a trifling matter for Avoch-Dar to use his magic to put an end to me there and then. But he devised an unkinder fate. He ordered me transported to Kyastor, a small island far out in the Opal Sea, which he had already taken. If you do not know of it, Kyastor is practically barren, but it has one precious resource. Gold. I was sentenced to a wretched existence working in the mines. This prospect depressed me so that I decided to end my life by casting myself overboard from the ship taking me there. It was then that I discovered how well I had been made. I found I could function perfectly without air for indefinite periods of time. Eventually, the tides brought me to these shores."

"A fanciful story indeed!" Meath sneered.

"Nevertheless it is true, sir. If you doubt it, perhaps you would care to have me demonstrate in yonder river?"

"I don't think you need do that, Tycho," Leandor said. "I for one am inclined to believe your tale. But what are we to do with you now?"

"If we can't kill it, leave it here," Meath suggested. "Our mission is hard enough without taking on every stray we meet."

"You are on a mission? My strength and stamina could be helpful to you. And I have a skill that might prove useful."

Shani was curious. "What is it?"

Tycho looked around. His gaze fell upon the saddles they had taken from their horses and laid on the grass. "Allow me to demonstrate."

He outstretched an arm. Nothing happened for a second or two. Then one of the saddles moved of its own accord. Slowly, it rose from the ground, reached a height equal to the top of a small tree and hung motionless in the air. When Tycho moved his arm from side to side the saddle moved too. It swung left to right, right to left, in a pendulum motion. When he lowered his arm, it sank back to the ground.

"Devilry!" Meath exclaimed. "What more proof do we need?"

"It is a small ability," Tycho explained, "a quite limited power of mind over matter. An idle trick used to entertain Avoch-Dar's court."

"We can't waste time arguing about this," Leandor decided. "I propose that Tycho comes with us, but strictly on probation. If he shows sign of treachery, we'll abandon him. Shani?"

"That seems fair."

"Meath?"

"I don't like it. But I suppose anything I have to say won't change your mind, will it, Leandor?"

Tycho said, "Thank you, sirs, madam. I will not betray your trust. Would it be possible to know a little more of your mission?"

Leandor told him something of their quest for the Book of Shadows and the perils defending it. "And I believe the cannibal tribe was probably one of them," he concluded.

"I would do anything to aid a plan that might overthrow my ex-master," the homunculus vowed.

After that, they fell to speculating about the demon race, although Meath took small part in the discussion.

"What puzzles me," Shani admitted, "is that if

the demon folk were so powerful, how did they vanish from the world?"

"I heard Avoch-Dar tell many stories about them," Tycho revealed. "It is said that their time was an age of wonders. They had undreamed of weapons that spat fire and could lay waste to a city in a day. And they commanded horseless chariots that transported them across land, and through the air too, in the blink of an eye. There is even a tale that they used a device to bring the stars near, yet it was no more than a tube of metal and glass that could be held in the hand."

"That sounds too fantastic to credit," Shani laughed. "But what of their end? Did you hear stories about that?"

"Many, my lady. One legend holds that they perished in terrible wars between themselves. Another says they used their awesome magic to fashion a gateway to another world and passed through it."

"Why would they do that?" Leandor said.

"Perhaps the coming of man made them leave. Who can say, my lord?"

"We'll probably never know," Leandor speculated. He changed the subject. "Look, Tycho, if you're going to accompany us, I at least would prefer you dropped this lord and lady business. It makes me feel uncomfortable."

Shani nodded agreement.

"I was created to serve. It is a difficult habit to break."

"I know. But we face danger equally and none should be higher or lower in the others' eyes. I don't think any of us would object to you using our names. Isn't that right, Meath?"

The mercenary grunted and turned away.

"That's Craigo Meath. This is Shani Vanya. And I'm Dal—"

"Oh, I know who *you* are, my ... I know who you are, Dalveen Leandor. I recognized you right away. Avoch-Dar spoke of the warrior called Nightshade many times. He detests you above all men."

After resting for a while, they made ready to leave. And for a few moments, Leandor and Shani found themselves alone by the river.

"Meath seems less than pleased with our new companion," Shani commented.

"He's a suspicious man by nature, and that's no bad thing under the circumstances. But I think we've made the right decision in letting Tycho accompany us."

"Have we? I'm not so sure."

"His story rang true. And he didn't have to rescue us, after all. To tell you the truth, Shani, I'd welcome any ally who aided us in our mission. I won't rest until I'm back in Allderhaven and –"

"And with your betrothed?"

"You know about Bethan, then?"

"Who hasn't heard about the great romance of Nightshade and his Princess Bethan?" She hesitated. "What kind of a person is she?"

"Quite different to me in many ways. But she's brave, and she certainly has a mind of her own. As well as having the sort of dignity and cultured ways you'd expect from a noble."

"I see," she sniffed. "Well, peasants like me wouldn't know anything about the nobility, would they?"

"Shani, I didn't mean –"

"No, of course you didn't," she said coldly. "I think it's time we went, don't you?"

He caught her arm. "Not before I say this. I was brought up with Bethan, and I owe her and her father a great deal. I repaid them by running away when they needed me most. I didn't see it like that at the time, but it's what it amounts to. Now Avoch-Dar holds Bethan hostage and the gods alone know what terrors await her. I hope that, as my friend, you'd want to help put that right."

"Yes, Dalveen," she said softly, "I do."

They rejoined the others and set off.

The river ran east, so they followed its course. Despite being on foot, Tycho had no trouble keeping up with them, and his energy seemed inexhaustible.

In a few hours the forest came to an end, and they moved into an area of lush, gentle greenness.

The sun was just beginning to set when they saw a woman standing on the riverbank.

The woman had her back to them. When she heard their approach she turned.

She was beautiful.

Flowing blonde hair framed a face of delicate perfection. Her long-lashed eyes were deepest hazel. Her nose and mouth were exquisitely formed. Her skin had the smoothness of finely polished marble.

She wore a simple white silk gown and her feet were bare. Yet the plainness of dress only underlined her elegance, and when she moved, it was with natural grace.

There was no surprise or fear in her expression. She regarded the travellers, even Tycho, with no more than mild curiosity. The warm, open smile she gave them showed teeth like gleaming pearls.

"Greetings. A fine day, is it not?" Her voice was gentle and pleasing.

Leandor hesitated, dumbfounded at coming upon so lovely a woman and her light talk of the weather. He glanced at Shani and Meath, and saw they looked taken aback, too. Tycho was impossible to read.

"Well met, my lady," Leandor finally managed. "And the day is indeed agreeable. May we dismount?"

"Of course, why not?"

They got off their horses, and Shani said, "I'm surprised at your casual attitude, given this land's dark reputation."

The woman laughed, soft and melodious. "You mustn't believe everything you hear about Zenobia. We aren't all rogues and monsters, you know."

"That hasn't exactly been our experience so far," Shani replied, her tone wary.

"Then you've been very unlucky. I'm sorry about that." The friendly smile came again. "Oh, how silly of me. Where are my manners? I am Aurora."

"I'm Shani Vanya, this is Dalveen Leandor, that's—"

"Craigo Meath, at your service, good lady," the mercenary interrupted. He bowed low, grinning.

Shani bit back a laugh and finished the introductions. "And our friend Tycho."

The shaggy creature bobbed his head respectfully. "My lady."

"Visitors are a rarity in these parts. Where are you bound?"

"East, roughly." Leandor was deliberately vague. "We have ... an appointment."

"It won't prevent you taking refreshments, I hope."

"To be honest, we've already been delayed and –"

"Nonsense! My home is very close, and I would be honoured to extend hospitality to you all."

"Well, we haven't eaten for a while..." Meath said.

"That's settled then. Come along."

She made her way toward a copse and they followed.

"Do we have time for social calls?" Shani hissed.

"Food and drink *would* be welcome," Leandor whispered. "And what is there to fear from a lone woman?"

"We should be wary of all we meet in this grim land," she reminded him.

"Granted. But if there's a chance she might help us in our quest, I'm for investigating. We won't linger and we'll stay alert, all right?"

Shani nodded in reluctant agreement.

Aurora beckoned and they hurried to catch up. She led them along a path that wound through a profusion of flowering plants before coming to a glade. Beyond trees heavy with fruit and blossom, beside a tinkling brook, stood a splendid villa. The spacious building was made of white stone. Fluted columns stood on either side of its entrance.

The cool interior was just as tasteful. Finely woven rugs were scattered across the marbled floors, rich tapestries and ornate carvings decorated the walls.

"Do you live here alone?" Shani asked.

"No, my sisters live with me." She indicated sofas heaped with plump cushions. "Make yourselves comfortable and I'll fetch them. I'm sure they'll be thrilled to know we have guests."

When she left, Meath said, "That woman has regal bearing. I'll wager she's of an aristocratic family."

"But why are she and her sisters living here in Zenobia, of all places?" Shani wondered. "And how do they protect themselves against the horrors of this land? There don't seem to be any servants or workers around."

"You should be grateful she's welcomed us so warmly, girl," Meath told her. "*I* think she's charming."

"And would you be of that opinion if she were less fair of form? It's often a mistake to be swayed by a pretty face, Meath."

He reddened, and was about to say something when Leandor cut in to avoid an argument between them. "Not now, you two. The only important thing is that we reach the book as soon as possible. Nothing must stand in the way of that. We'll stay here only as long as politeness dictates."

At that moment Aurora returned, arm in arm with two women equally as beautiful as herself. Each had the same creamy skin, blonde hair and hazel eyes. They were dressed almost identically, and it looked as though no more than a couple of years separated their ages.

"These are my sisters," Aurora announced, "Abigail and Adela."

They had the same winning smiles too.

The refreshments turned out to be a banquet.

Countless superbly prepared dishes were laid before them. Platters of red meat, fowl and fish in pungent sauces. Bowls of steamed and raw vegetables with exotic dressings. Several varieties of newly baked breads. A selection of sweet puddings, cheeses and fruit. Juices, mead and mellow wines flowed freely.

Leandor, Shani and Meath were slightly embarrassed by the extravagant offering. Tycho, needing neither food nor drink, sat quietly on one side.

Explaining that they had eaten earlier, the sisters did not share the meal either. But they did serve it.

"I'm afraid there are no servants," apologized Abigail as she cleared away the last of the dishes.

"The truth is that we have fallen on hard times since the death of our father," Adela said.

"But our needs are humble," Aurora added, "and somehow we manage."

"In that case we're all the more grateful for your generosity," Leandor replied. "The food was wonderful."

"From where have you come?" Adela asked.

"Delgarvo," Shani answered. "Have you ever been there?"

"Oh, *no*!" the sisters chorused, giggling.

"We have never left Zenobia," Aurora said. "Nor would we wish to. We have everything we need here."

"Did you know this land is considered evil by outsiders?"

"Yes," Abigail responded, "and we think it's ridiculous, don't we?"

Her sisters nodded vigorously.

"Everything we've seen so far has only confirmed that this is a bad place," Shani continued. "You must be aware that you have some ... well, odd neighbours?"

Adela adopted a serious expression. "We can't deny that. But there are no such goings-on in these parts."

"We lead a quiet, peaceful life and no one bothers us," Aurora stated. "You have to understand that our family has lived here for generations and is highly respected. We have little to do with outsiders, or they with us."

"How big a family is it?" Meath wanted to know.

"Just us," Aurora replied. "We are the last of our line."

"You have no husbands?"

The giggling broke out again.

"There is a shortage of such in this area," blushed Abigail. "Not that we mind. We are quite happy as we are."

"Tell me," Leandor said, "if we continue to follow the river, will it take us eastward?"

"Yes," Aurora confirmed. "It bends and twists, but finally reaches the far coast."

"Good." He started to rise. "We should be going."

"*No!*" the sisters protested with one voice.

"It's dark now," Adela explained, "and not a good time to be travelling."

"But you just said –"

"*This* area is safe, certainly. It's a different story once you're away from here. So it would be much better for you to stay a while."

Abigail chimed in with, "You must stay the night. We insist!"

"One night won't make any difference, Leandor," Meath suggested. "And we need the rest."

"We do. I suppose if we don't leave it too late to start out tomorrow... Yes, why not? Agreed, Shani?"

She nodded, yawning.

"How about you, Tycho?"

"I am happy to abide by your decision, si ... Dalveen."

Aurora stood. "Excellent. If you follow me I will show you your rooms."

"Hard times? Humble needs?" Shani mocked. "There's precious little evidence of either around here."

They were gathered in her room to discuss the day's events before turning in.

"You're being unfair to them," Meath argued.

"Perhaps. But their constant prattling and giggling was getting on my nerves." She sighed. "I suppose I'm just tired."

"We all are," Leandor said. "I'm for bed. By the way, Tycho, can you do without sleep as well as food?"

"Yes. In fact, I have never slept. But I welcome the hours of darkness. They are a good time to think in peace. And tonight I shall be thinking about the mystery of this house."

"What do you mean?"

"What we have learned of these women puzzles me. As Shani pointed out earlier, how do they survive here unmolested? I find their story about being left alone because they are a respected family hard to credit. I cannot see the flesh-eating tribesmen, for example, showing much respect for anyone. And how do the sisters support themselves? They say they have no servants. Do they plant crops or raise cattle or catch fish? Judging by the softness of their hands, I would say not."

"I didn't notice that," Leandor admitted.

"Then you probably didn't notice their toes either."

"Their toes?" Meath exclaimed. "By Eldrick's beard, what have their *toes* got to do with it, you fuzzy moron?"

Tycho ignored the jibe. "I observed that the middle toe of each of their feet was longer than the others. That is significant, I believe. But I cannot recall why. Unfortunately, my memory is no better or worse than a human's. I shall do my best to remember during the night."

Leandor didn't know whether to take Tycho seriously. "One thing I did notice," he told them, "was that none of our rooms have locks. It might be a good idea to secure the doors in some way before retiring. Now let's get some rest."

They filed out and left Shani to sleep.

She took the room's only chair and propped its backrest under the door handle. Then she stretched out on the bed fully clothed and fell into exhausted slumber.

It was hard to tell whether minutes or hours had passed when the noise woke her.

Chapter 12

Shani realized the noise that woke her was coming from the door. The handle rattled and there was a thudding against the wood.

She snatched a knife and crossed the room. The pounding grew more determined, making the propped chair shake. Her first thought was to go out and confront whatever was on the other side. But she decided against it when she heard a scraping sound.

Her night visitor was scratching at the door.

Shani threw her weight against it. For a moment, the pressure from outside became so great she feared the door wouldn't hold. She pushed with all her might.

Suddenly the assault stopped. What could have been wheezing or heavy breathing took its place. It was followed by muffled footsteps moving away.

She stayed where she was, ear to the door. Then the brief silence was broken by another commotion along the corridor. More pounding and scratching went on for a few seconds before the footsteps came again, past her room and down the stairs.

Taking a deep breath, she shoved aside the chair and reached for the handle. She inched open the door. A series of long gouges ran down the outside, exposing fresh wood beneath. Knife raised, she poked her head out and looked up and down the corridor.

There was movement and she stiffened. But it was Leandor, coming towards her. He moved stealthily, sword ready.

"Are you all right, Shani?"

"Yes, but something tried to get into my room."

"Mine, too."

"Did you see it?"

"No." He glanced at the scratch marks. "It did similar damage to my door though."

"I'm sure it went downstairs, Dalveen."

"We'll check. But let's see if the others are all right first."

Tycho appeared. "I heard sounds," he said. "Is all well?"

"Something got into the house," Leandor told him.

Shani knocked at Meath's door. He answered it sleepily. "What is it? What happened?"

"An intruder," she informed him. "Did you see or hear anything?"

"No, I didn't. I slept through the whole thing."

"We think whatever it was went downstairs," Leandor said. "We'll look. You and Tycho search up here. And be careful. If those scratches are anything to go by, it's dangerous. Come on, Shani."

When they got to the bottom of the stairs they found the front door open. A quick look showed the rooms on the ground floor were empty, so they warily stepped outside the house.

There was a full moon. It bathed the landscape in eerie silver.

Shani spotted a grey shape over by the copse. "See that, Dalveen?"

"Yes, but I can't quite make out... Look, it's moving!"

It streaked across their line of vision, left to right. The light wasn't good enough to make out what it was, but it was large and ran on all fours. Before it disappeared into the darkness they had the fleeting impression of an elongated head.

"It's certainly a beast of some kind," Leandor said.

A high-pitched howl came from the trees, a

drawn-out wailing cry that turned their blood to ice.

"What's wrong?"

They spun around. Aurora stood in the doorway holding a candle. Shani and Leandor breathed a sigh of relief.

"Something got into the house," he told her. "Some sort of animal."

"Are you sure? I didn't hear anything."

"Positive," Shani replied, irritated that the woman should doubt them. "We just saw it. And you'll find it did some damage upstairs. Has anything like this happened before?"

Aurora looked puzzled. "No. There aren't any wild animals around here. And how could it have got in?"

They examined the door. There were no signs of it being broken into or forced in any way.

"Might it have been left open?" Leandor asked.

"I expect that must have been it," Aurora decided. "How silly of us."

"Do you know if your sisters saw anything?"

"Not them. They've always been heavy sleepers. And as everything seems to be all right now, I don't see any point in disturbing them, do you?"

All they could do after that was make sure the front entrance was secure and go back to their rooms.

* * *

The rest of the night passed without incident.

When Leandor and the others went down early the next morning, Abigail and Adela greeted them. They had a substantial breakfast ready, but didn't eat themselves.

"Did you know something strange occurred during the night?" Leandor said.

They nodded in unison.

"Did either of you see anything?"

"No," Adela replied. "We'd sleep through an earthquake. All we know is what Aurora told us."

"We think it was an animal," Shani told them.

"Well, the occasional wild dog has been known to wander into this area and it could have been one of those," Abigail speculated. "But we haven't seen any around here for years. It's a mystery to us."

"Where *is* Aurora?" Meath asked.

"She has business to attend to today," Adela explained. "She'll be back later. As a matter of fact, we're going to have to leave you ourselves for a while."

"We were going to set off again this morning," Leandor said.

"Just wait until we get back. We want to give you some provisions for your journey."

"Thank you, Adela, but that won't be necessary. We really should be on our way."

"We insist. We don't like the idea of you going without enough food and drink for your journey."

"We'll hang on for a *little* while, then."

Abigail smiled. "Good! Make the house your own. Oh, and we watered and fed your horses, so you won't need to worry about that."

They said their goodbyes and left.

Leandor watched them go, then turned to Tycho. "You were right about their toes. I looked. Have you remembered the significance of it yet?"

"I'm afraid not. The uproar last night interrupted my train of thought. But it will come to me, I'm sure."

"Something else funny about last night was how long it took Aurora to put in an appearance," Shani commented.

"Yes," Meath agreed. "And none of them seem particularly disturbed at the thought of a ravening beast loose in their home."

Shani grinned. "Oh, you're starting to see beyond their comely faces, are you?"

Leandor cut short the bickering with, "As we're going to be here a bit longer, I've got an idea. While the sisters are out, why don't you and I scout the area for sign of the animal, Meath? We might find tracks. It could be useful to know what we're up against."

The mercenary nodded. "All right. I could use some exercise anyway."

"And Tycho and I can get together what we need for our departure," Shani said.

It didn't take them long to gather their few possessions. So Shani decided to kill time by resting in her room. Tycho left her in peace and went to his own.

She was half dozing, about an hour later, when she heard the door slam below. Assuming either Leandor and Meath or the sisters had returned, she didn't bother moving.

Then there was the sound of something breaking downstairs. Almost immediately there was a heavy crash, as though a piece of furniture had been overturned.

Shani got up and crept to the door. She went to the stairwell and looked over, but saw nothing out of the ordinary. Tycho came out of his room and she held a finger to her lips. He understood and kept silent.

She whispered in his ear, "I'm going to investigate. I'll call you if it's clear."

Drawing a knife, she tiptoed down the stairs.

The front door was closed. A large wooden cabinet lay on its side by the far wall. Shards of broken pottery from a vase were scattered around it. Everything else seemed to be all right.

If she hadn't turned at that moment she would probably have died.

Chapter 13

The thing coming at her looked like a wolf.

But it was bigger than any she had ever seen. And it walked on its hind legs.

Its slitty yellow eyes were pitiless. The chasm of a mouth displayed horribly pointed fangs. A drawling tongue lolled over its thin lips. Outstretched paws bristled with murderously sharp talons.

Bent forward with hunched back, the creature panted wetly.

Shani screamed.

One of the massive paws swiped at her head. She ducked, somehow avoiding the lethal slash, close enough that she felt a slap of air as it passed.

Remembering the knife in her hand, she lashed out wildly. The creature fell back from the blade, moving with frightening speed, then lurched in again snapping its jaws.

She tried to get out of its way. Throwing herself to the side, she struck a low table and crashed to the floor. Winded, she rolled on to her back. The snarling beast loomed over her. Clutching the knife in both hands, Shani jabbed at its face, narrowly missing the snout as it pulled away.

Scrambling to her feet, she managed to put a little distance between them. The wolf-thing charged. She drew back her arm and flung the knife.

It was a close miss, but a miss nevertheless. The blade skimmed past the monster and buried itself in the door. Shani swiftly pulled another knife from her sleeve. Then she side-stepped to avoid the approaching nightmare. The creature smashed a chair out of its way and kept coming.

Panting from terror and exhaustion, she dashed for the staircase. The beast swerved, dropped to all fours and loped after her. Shani was on the steps when it caught up. It pawed at her, entangling its claws in the back of her jerkin. She kicked out and tried to shrug off the garment.

"Shani!"

Tycho thundered down the stairs, making them tremble under the weight of his hefty body. He took her shoulders and wrenched her toward him. The jerkin ripped, freeing her. He continued to tug, dragging her up several more steps, then moved to place himself between her and the beastly attacker.

The enraged creature half rose and slashed at him. It would have meant death for a human. But the blow struck the metal band around his waist. Two of the monster's claws snapped on impact. Yelping, it jerked back.

Shani took advantage of its confusion. She lurched downward and plunged her blade into its paw. The wolf-thing shrieked in pain. Whimpering, it turned and limped for the door.

Which at that moment opened.

Leandor and Meath came in. They froze at the sight of the monstrous creature racing their way. It knocked against Meath, smashing him into the wall. And it was through the entrance before Leandor had his sword half drawn. He ran after it. Meath picked himself up and followed.

They returned almost immediately.

"It moved too fast for us, despite the wound," Leandor reported. "Are you all right, Shani?"

"Yes, thanks to Tycho." She smiled at the artificial creature. "Just a bit shaky. But I managed to inflict some damage on the thing."

"What *was* it?" Meath said. "It looked like a wolf, but it was too big and ... *wrong*, somehow."

"I believe I can answer that question," Tycho told them.

"I wish you would." Leandor slammed the door and saw Shani's knife sticking in it. He and Meath walked over to the others.

"The experience we have just had confirms a theory I was beginning to work out," Tycho explained. "That creature was a were-beast. In this case it took the form of a wolf. It could as easily have been a leopard, hyena, hunter-lizard or any of a number of other savage animals. And there is one sign of humans capable of transforming themselves in such a way."

"Which is?" Shani asked.

"They have elongated middle toes."

"You can't mean the sisters!" Meath blurted out.

"I'm afraid so. At least one, probably all, is a were-beast. The correct word for the condition is lycanthropy. Sometimes the lycanthrope has no control over it, and the transformation is triggered by a full moon. But as this attack took place in daylight, I suspect these women can change at will."

"So they are evil in nature?" Leandor asked.

"Perhaps. They may have made a pact with dark forces and became were-beasts in exchange for immortality. Or inherited their plight from ancestors. It is said to run in the blood of some families. There is even a legend that drinking rainwater from the paw print of a wolf will pass on the infection."

"There's another possibility," Leandor suggested. "Which is that they were made the way they are by the demon race, to ensnare anyone seeking the book."

"Yes," Tycho agreed, "this may well be another peril. In any event, the sisters are under a curse, slaves to a terrible blood-lust that only freshly-killed meat can satisfy. Preferably human."

"That explains the slaughtered sheep we found," Meath commented.

"What?" Shani said.

"When we were out, we found tracks, but they were too indistinct to identify what made them. They lead to the bodies of several wild sheep. Their throats had been torn to shreds and their blood drained."

"When a were-beast cannot find human prey," Tycho pointed out, "it will make do with animals as second best. The thing to remember is that these creatures are cunning. They may have had centuries to perfect their hunting techniques. And they are almost invulnerable. You were lucky, Shani. Ordinary weapons can hurt them, but never kill them." He noticed something on a nearby rug and reached for it. "If any of you have doubts about the true nature of these women, this should dispel them. Two claws broke off when the creature raked me. And now we have this." He held up the object for them to see.

It was a long fragment of human fingernail.

"You mean, separated from the body, the claws went back to their normal appearance?" Leandor said.

"Precisely. If they were to die while in the guise of were-beasts, the women would revert to human form."

"I'm for getting out of here," Meath decided. "But suppose we run into them before then? You said our weapons are of no real use."

"Ancient lore states that werewolves are creatures of the moon goddess. Silver is the precious metal associated with the moon, and is said to be the only thing that can destroy them. Have you noticed that among all the precious items in this house, none are made of silver?"

"I imagine none of us has any either," Leandor observed.

Meath and Shani shook their heads.

"I do," Tycho said. He indicated the steely band at his waist. "This is solid silver, one of the elements necessary to give me life. It would take only a small amount to have an effect on a werewolf. I would be pleased to donate some."

"But how best to use it?" Meath wondered.

Shani drew a knife. "Simple. Silver's fairly soft and can be worked quite easily. We heat it in the hearth, beat it out and wrap it around a couple of my blades. Then we'd have something to defend ourselves with."

"Good idea," Leandor congratulated her. "Let's get started."

Meath kept watch while Shani lit a fire and found a copper bowl. Leandor used the edge of his sword to scrape shavings of the bright material from Tycho's body. They were careful not to take too much lest it prove vital to their friend's well-being.

Once heated, there turned out to be enough of the pliant metal to treat three blades. They left them to cool.

"Remember," Shani reminded her companions, "adding the silver increases the weight of the knives and alters their balance. That means they may not throw accurately. So aim higher than normal, to allow for dip, and give it as much force as possible. It might be better to use them as daggers."

"Let's hope we don't have to use them at all," Leandor replied. "Here, they've hardened. We'll take one each. Then we're getting out of here."

He tucked one in his belt. Shani took another for her arm holster. Meath slipped the third into his boot and went back to stand by the door.

Just as he reached it he called, "Watch out! They're coming!"

Chapter 14

"It's Adela and Aurora," Meath reported as he hurried to rejoin the others. "There's no sign of Abigail. What do we do?"

"Nothing," Leandor told them. "We stay calm and take our leave as planned. I want to avoid bloodshed if possible, but keep your knives within reach."

The door swung open and the sisters bustled in, smiling, each with a small basket over their arm. They looked shocked when they saw the damage.

"What happened?" gasped Aurora.

Leandor had to admit it was a good performance. "Our mysterious visitor came back."

"Was anyone hurt?" Adela asked, wide-eyed.

"Only the wolf," Shani replied.

"Wolf?" Aurora made a show of appearing baffled. "Surely not. There aren't any for miles."

"It was certainly wolf-*like*," Leandor explained, "and big."

"Wolves died out in this area many years ago," she claimed, "and the few we saw as children were never very large."

"But we must apologize for this outrage," Adela said. "You are our guests, after all."

"Not for much longer, I'm afraid. We're about to leave."

The sisters acted disappointed.

"Where's Abigail, by the way?" Meath wondered.

Aurora's smile wavered for a split second. "She's been ... unwell. But she'll be along soon."

Adela laid the baskets in front of them. "We've brought some fresh fruit for your journey. And we have one or two other things, some little gifts, so you must wait while we get them." They headed for the door. "We'll only be a few minutes," she called on the way out.

"They're setting us up for something," Meath said darkly.

"Why don't we just go?" suggested Shani.

"Yes," Leandor agreed, "this cat and mouse game has gone on long enough. Ready, Tycho?"

"Certainly, Dalveen. But we should proceed with care. Trickery is second nature with these creatures."

They walked to the door, opened it, and found themselves facing Abigail.

She quickly adopted her usual grin. "You're not going without saying goodbye, I hope?"

Leandor glanced at her right hand. It was wrapped in a bandage. The others noticed, too. "I see you've hurt yourself," he said.

"Oh, this." She tried to sound casual. "It's nothing. Just a burn." The hand disappeared behind her back and she changed the subject. "My sisters tell me you were bothered by a wild animal."

"Yes. It was something like a wolf. And it did a bit more than bother us."

Abigail surveyed the wrecked furniture. "So I see. It's terribly worrying. I mean, what would we have done if you hadn't been here?"

"I think you would have managed," Shani said coldly.

"Three defenceless women, living alone? I'm not sure we could." She appealed directly to Leandor. "Won't you consider staying a little longer, in case it comes back?"

"I'm sorry, Abigail, we must be moving on."

"Please? Just one more day."

"We can't."

"How can you leave us," she pleaded, "with something awful on the prowl?"

"We've delayed too long already, and –"

"You *can't* go!" The cheerful mask fell away. Her voice was angry, demanding. *"We won't let you!"*

"Have a care, Dalveen!" Tycho warned.

Leandor stepped back from the enraged woman.

"You will not leave here!" She was shouting now, and seemed to be losing control. *"You ... will ... not... Will* not ... *leave!"*

Abigail's face twisted horribly. The calm beauty drained out of it. Her shrill words gave way to a heavy, panting wheeze.

They watched, transfixed, as she rapidly began to alter.

It started with her eyes. Their roundness flowed into slits. The pupils turned black, the whites flooded with sickly yellow.

The skin on her face, neck and arms grew numerous dark spots. They instantly sprouted into patches of coarse hair that spread to form a dense fur covering. The flesh from her chin to the bridge of her nose took on a fluid appearance, then erupted outwards into a snout. Her mouth stretched and widened as teeth became fangs.

They heard the moist cracking noise of bones contorting into different shapes. Abigail, hardly recognizable as human any longer, stooped forward, jutting shoulder blades slicing through the back of her dress. The rest of the fabric burst apart under the strain of an expanding body. Sinewy muscles rippled below the surface of her fuzzy hide. Her hands swelled to paws, shreds of bandage hanging from one set of talons.

A total transformation had taken place.

The slavering beast gave a throaty growl. Flecks of saliva dappled its lower jaw. It regarded the four companions slyly.

Leandor slipped the knife from his belt. Panting, the were-creature raised its claws, ready to pounce. Shani and Meath took up defensive positions, knives outstretched.

The savage eyes of the thing that had been a woman seconds before flicked from face to face.

Then suddenly it sprang at Meath.

He quickly fell back, slashing with his dagger. But it was a fake attack. The cunning beast turned with incredible speed and went for Leandor instead. It was a ploy that almost worked. Leandor's reflexes, honed by a lifetime of combat, served to avoid the deadly swipe by a hair's breadth. And as he dodged aside he struck out with his knife, missing, but close enough to fend off the creature.

Meath and Shani advanced, their swinging blades harrying it from front and side. Leandor joined in on the opposite flank, leaving only a gap at the monster's rear. Arms stretched out, Tycho moved to cut off this escape route. The beast lashed wildly at the encircling warriors, maddened at the sight of threatening silver.

Neither side could get near enough to do real damage to the other. It was a stalemate.

Shani decided to break it.

Clutching the knife by its blade, her hand went back until the hilt was over her shoulder. "*Give me room!*" she yelled.

The others scattered.

She remembered her own advice, aimed high and threw hard.

The knife smacked into the furry chest. An unholy scream pierced the air, part human, part bestial. Pain and fury mingled in it.

The werewolf pawed at the knife, stumbled, and crashed to the floor.

A great outrush of breath escaped its lungs. Then the body convulsed, and was still.

They approached cautiously. Already the beast's features were melting away. In death, the fur seemed to evaporate; the limbs relaxed and went back to human form. The wolfish maw and snout dissolved, the eyes became round again. Claws shrank, leaving normal hands and feet.

The beast had gone. They looked down on a beautiful young woman. Had it not been for the knife projecting from the tatters of her dress, she could have been sleeping.

"Good throw, Shani," Leandor said.

"Seeing her like this, I'm not sure I deserve congratulating. She looks so ... peaceful."

"Feel no regrets," Tycho told her. "You have released this woman from a dreadful curse."

"Don't go soft on us now, girl," Meath added. "Think of all the lives she and her sisters must have taken."

"Talking of her sisters," Leandor remembered, "I wonder where—"

The front door crashed open.

Aurora and Adela appeared. They saw Abigail. Pure hatred filled their faces.

Their bodies started to mutate.

"You'll pay for this!" Adela spat.

"We'll tear your *hearts* out!" shrieked Aurora.

Meath rushed at them. "Come on! Before they change!"

He was too late. The other side of the room was only a few paces away, but that was enough for the sisters to complete their transformation.

The Aurora were-beast attacked immediately. A lighting-fast paw slash caught the charging mercenary's arm, laying open his sleeve. His knife flew out of his hand and he lost his footing. The beast hovered over him as he tried to hold it off with kicking legs and swinging fists.

The Adela creature made for Leandor and Shani. It reached them with such speed that Shani had no time to pluck her knife from Abigail's corpse. She dived to one side, hoping to reach Meath's blade, but the way was blocked by his struggle with Aurora.

Leandor was taking the full brunt of Adela's fury. He had to draw on every ounce of his fighting skill to keep away the razor-sharp talons and fangs.

Then luck favoured him. His dagger nicked the creature's arm. Had it been an ordinary weapon the cut wouldn't have mattered. But the touch of the silver-swathed blade was agonizing to the werewolf. It roared with pain and the arm went up.

Leandor darted beneath it and thrust the knife into the creature's hairy torso. It collapsed whimpering.

Shani was still trying to get Meath's weapon. A task made more urgent by the fact that the mercenary was obviously weakening under the assault.

When he yelled for help she decided to go to his aid anyway, even without the silver blade.

"*Shani!*" It was Tycho. "Be ready!" He pointed to Meath's knife.

She didn't understand what he meant. Then she saw him close his eyes and lift his hand, as he had in the forest.

The knife rose from the floor. It hung in the air for a second, rocking gently, before gliding in her direction. When it arrived overhead she leapt and grabbed it.

Aurora's grotesque back wasn't a difficult target for someone with Shani's talent. She put all her force behind the throw, striking the beast below its left shoulder blade.

Meath just managed to roll clear before the mortally wounded creature toppled over. Its head landed with a crack next to his, and he felt its last gasp of fetid breath against his face.

In dying, Adela and Aurora, like their sister, returned to human appearance.

Leandor and Tycho helped Meath to his feet. Shani gently rolled his sleeve and examined the wound. "I don't think it's too bad," she announced. "Hold still and I'll bind it."

"I should, er... I should thank you," Meath said with a certain reluctance.

"You're welcome," she replied, tearing a strip of cloth for a bandage. "And don't you think Tycho deserves thanks, too?"

Meath hesitated, sour-faced, before mumbling something none of them caught.

"Pardon? I couldn't quite hear that."

"I said..." He sighed. "I said ... thank you, Tycho."

The homunculus gave a small bow. "Glad to be of assistance."

Leandor smiled. "All right. When this is done

we'll take what we need and get out of here. But I don't think it'll be necessary to burn the place down this time, do you, Meath?"

"You read my mind. Pity. *Ouch!*"

"Sorry," Shani said innocently. "Did that hurt?"

Chapter 15

Torpoint was heavy with the stench of death. Bodies were being cleared from the palace's battle-ravaged corridors.

Heedless of the carnage, Avoch-Dar swept past, accompanied by his personal guard. They strode to the King's council chamber and threw open its great doors. Every one of the score of seated counsellors inside had an armed sentry at his back.

Fearful eyes turned the magician's way.

Avoch-Dar stood at the head of the massive table. He made a show of slowly removing his black gauntlets as he gazed at each of their ashen faces in turn.

Casually he dropped one of the armoured gloves on to the oak surface. Several of those present flinched at the loud smack it made.

"So this is Eldrick's famous Council of Elders," the sorcerer mocked. He tossed down the other gauntlet. "And elder is obviously an apt description. I see nothing but white beards and leathery skin. I hear the creak of ancient bones and blood thin as water coursing through crusty veins."

A red-faced counsellor at the far end of the table shouted, "You have no respect for the wisdom of age!"

The sorcerer snapped his fingers, almost carelessly, and a small, intensely green fireball streaked at the man. It struck his raised hand and dissolved in a puff of mist. He yelped in pain, falling back in his chair to rub at the scalded flesh. His colleagues gasped and kept silent.

"You are correct," Avoch-Dar calmly agreed, "I have no respect for this so-called governing body. And even less for a king weak enough to heed its advice." He turned to a group of guards and snapped, "Bring Eldrick and the Princess to me now!" They hastened to obey.

"But you, gentlemen, are about to perform your last public function," the magician continued. A servant passed him a sheet of parchment. "This is the treaty of surrender. You will sign it."

The guards returned with Bethan. She walked proudly with her head held high.

"Ah, Your Royal Highness." Avoch-Dar gave a bow of sham courtesy. "You are just in time to witness the transfer of power."

She glared at him. "You won't get away with this, you viper."

He laughed scornfully. "Oh, but I already have, my dear. This document seals my victory."

"Since when have you needed a treaty to take what you want?"

"If the citizens of Delgarvo know that your father and his council have formally handed me the throne they will more readily accept my rule."

"They'll never *accept you, tyrant! The people will not rest until you are overthrown!"*

"This piece of paper will hold them in check for the time being. Soon my magical powers will increase a thousand-fold, and then nothing they can do could possibly hurt me."

Before she could reply the King was marched in. Even in chains and herded at sword point, his regal manner was unmistakable. Despite his age, his broad back was straight, his eyes clear and cool.

"Father!" She ran and threw her arms around him.

"Are you all right, child?"

"Yes, he has not harmed me."

"How touching," sneered Avoch-Dar.

The King's chest swelled. His bound fists clenched. "If you lay a hand on my daughter –"

"You'll do what, *old man?" He laughed in the monarch's face. "But you need not trouble yourself on that account. Bethan has a part to play in my plan."*

"Never!" she stated defiantly.

"We'll see," the magician replied. "Meanwhile, we have business to conduct." He held up the treaty and addressed the room. "My terms are simple. I am your conqueror and you have no rights. Now each of you will sign."

"I will not lend my name to such an agreement," Eldrick declared.

"Then you'll watch as every man here is put to death. The choice is yours."

"You may get your way for now," Bethan told him, "but there's someone you won't be able to overcome so easily."

"Ah yes, Nightshade. No, I haven't forgotten your beloved Dalveen Leandor." He grinned spitefully. "But unfortunately for you his life is drawing to a close. Expect no help from that quarter, my lady."

"You lie," she whispered, tears welling in her eyes.

Avoch-Dar ignored her and thrust the treaty at King Eldrick. "I accept your unconditional surrender," he said.

"Surely you have *some* idea of where the book is to be found?" Meath asked again.

"No," Leandor repeated. "All Melva said was to travel east. And to trust my instincts."

"That's too vague. How will we *know*, man?"

"We'll know. I'm not sure how, but we will."

Shani returned from the water's edge with a damp cloth to tend Meath's arm. They were two days ride from the sisters' villa, and the river they followed had grown broader and faster-flowing.

"Where's Tycho?" she said.

Leandor nodded toward the bend upstream. "He decided to take a look round there. I told him not to go too far."

She peeled away the bandage on Meath's wound and gently dabbed at it. "It's healing nicely. I think you can leave the dressing off now."

"Good. We were just talking about how we'll know when we've reached the book's hiding place. Any ideas?"

"Not really. Except that if there's truth in the prophecy, and in some way Dalveen was meant to undertake this quest, it seems logical we'll recognize the place when we come to it."

"There are hardly going to be signposts, are there? I mean, in a land this size we could spend the rest of our lives searching."

"All I know is that Melva told me to travel eastward, and to trust my instincts," Leandor told him. "If you can come up with a better plan, let's hear it."

Meath didn't reply.

Shani broke the silence. "Here comes Tycho, and he looks in a hurry."

The artificial man arrived at a brisk pace. "There is something interesting yonder," he said.

Leandor stood. "What is it?"

"Ruins of some kind. Come, I'll show you."

Leading their horses, they followed him round the curving bank. The landside vegetation, on their right, was much thicker here, and the plentiful trees were tall. But there was a spot where the plant life had died back, revealing a section of masonry wall.

Meath touched the brickwork. Powdery red dust stained his fingertips. "It's old and starting to crumble. But it was well-built."

"Let's see what's on the other side," Leandor suggested, pushing into the bushes.

Beyond the fragment of wall they found a woodland. And as their eyes adjusted to the shade they began to make out other remains. More decayed walls, piles of granite blocks and the foundations of long-vanished buildings were recognizable, although almost entirely covered by undergrowth. Shani stepped over what looked like a tree trunk. When she raked aside the foliage she realized it was a toppled stone column.

"Look!" Tycho exclaimed. "Just above the tree line."

The tops of several tall buildings were visible.

"I don't think they're too far away," Leandor judged. "Follow me." He led them deeper into the wood.

The further they walked, the denser became the overgrown ruins. Soon there were fewer trees and the ground began to slope upwards. Then they were climbing a steep hill. Leandor was the first to reach its crest.

Shani caught up with him and asked, "What kind of settlement do you think this was?"

"It was more than a settlement." He pointed down the other side of the hill.

She turned, saw the view and gasped.

Meath and Tycho arrived, and took in the scene. "Fascinating!" the homunculus declared.

An ancient city stood in the valley below.

Buildings spread out as far as they could see. They varied from low and squat to elegant structures many stories high. Half-collapsed towers rose from places smothered by creeping greenery. Immense spires punched skyward. Others ended in jagged shapes like broken teeth. In places the outlines of roads could be seen through the jungle of vegetation.

"By the look of it," Meath said, "the place has been uninhabited for ages."

"Perhaps *this* is where the book's hidden," Shani said.

"Let's get down there and investigate," Leandor suggested. "But remember, there may still be perils to face. Stay alert."

Time and the elements had taken their toll.

Corruption was all around. Heaps of rubble

were strewn across many of the streets, making them impassable. Disintegrating walls tilted at crazy angles. Thick vines had burrowed through the paving stones, choking entire avenues with a prickly barrier.

And the silence was absolute.

But some parts of the city had fared better than others. Here and there, they came across areas that seemed intact, with stretches of road untouched by decay. After many wrong turns and dead ends, their wanderings took them into a great central square. Impressive buildings, in various stages of dilapidation, lined its four sides.

In the middle of the square about two dozen statues had been erected. Although a few had fallen, and one or two had suffered erosion, most were whole. The majority were warriors, holding swords and shields, with ornate plumed helmets on their heads. A handful of the sculptures depicted robed dignitaries who may have been politicians or statesmen.

"It crossed my mind that this might have been a demon city," Shani admitted, "but they're definitely human figures."

"That thought occurred to me, too," Meath agreed. "I wonder what happened to the people who lived here. Do you think the demons could have driven them out, or killed them?"

"Perhaps," Leandor said. "Assuming this place

is old enough to have been in existence at the same time the demons were. Ancient as it obviously is, it was probably built long after."

Shani took in their surroundings. A couple of the buildings had conical roofs. One was shaped like a corkscrew. "Whoever they were, their architecture was certainly bizarre. I've never seen anything quite like it."

"It is indeed a mystery," Tycho said, "and if my understanding of human nature is correct, solving mysteries gives your race great pleasure."

Leandor smiled. "Sometimes, yes. But I doubt we'd ever get to the bottom of what happened *here.* This place is unlike any city I've ever seen."

"We may be able to solve a minor puzzle or two, however," the homunculus stated. "And I believe we could do worse than starting there." He indicated the largest and best preserved building in the square. "It is a magnificent structure, and from its size, obviously had an important function of some sort."

They tied up their horses and went to climb the broad stone steps. If the enormous entrance had ever had doors, they must have decomposed long ago.

Inside it was gloomy, but they had no need to use one of their precious flints to make light. A huge hole in the high-domed ceiling provided just enough to see by. Before them was row after row of shelving, at least twice their height, arranged in straight lines. The shelves were packed with cylindrical objects, like tubes, giving a honeycomb effect.

"You know what this is, don't you?" Meath said. "A *library!* What luck! We could be at the end of our quest!"

He moved to the nearest shelf and took one of the scrolls. It crumbled to dust as he tried to open it. Leandor and Shani began investigating. Every roll of parchment they touched fell to pieces.

"Over here!" Tycho called from one side. "I've found some actual books."

But none could be handled without turning to powder.

Shani sighed. "It's ironic, really. The shelves survived because they're made of stone." She rubbed a finger against one. "Marble, I think. But the paper they held couldn't escape decaying. Think of all the knowledge that's been lost!"

"To hell with *that*!" Meath exclaimed. "What about the book we're after?"

"We can organize a proper search," Leandor said, "but don't be too hopeful of finding it."

"Why not?" the mercenary asked.

"Because I can't believe the demons would have left something so precious to rot in a place like this."

"You could be right. But we seek no ordinary

book. If it's as powerful as you say, perhaps it *wouldn't* rot."

"I still think they would have made sure it was better protected. It just doesn't seem logical that we'd find the book so easily. But maybe we should split up and—"

"Excuse me, Dalveen," Tycho interrupted. "Did any of you hear something just then?"

They shook their heads.

"My hearing is somewhat keener than a human's, and I could have sworn... Yes! Listen."

This time they heard it. The sound was of stone against stone, as though chunks of rock were being slowly ground together. They couldn't tell where it was coming from.

"What do you think it is, Tycho?" Shani whispered.

"I couldn't say. However, the thought occurs that we have entered a building that has probably been undisturbed for centuries. It might be –"

"That it's about to collapse," Leandor finished for him. "Outside, everybody. *Fast!*"

They hurried through the door and down the steps. When they were at a safe distance they stopped to watch. Nothing happened to the library.

Then they heard the rasping noise again. It was much louder this time.

And it came from behind them.

Chapter 16

Everything in the square looked exactly as before.

The statues in the centre kept their blank-eyed vigil over the same desolate scene.

"Could it be some other building that's about to go?" Meath asked.

"Quite possibly," Tycho replied. "In a place this old, many of them must be unsafe."

"Or maybe we're not alone here after all," Shani said.

The noise came again. Once more it sounded like stone being ground or scraped. And it was close. But they couldn't see where it came from.

"What in hell-fire is going on?" Meath exclaimed.

Leandor drew his sword. "Just keep your wits sharp and stand ready."

Shani and the mercenary followed his example, slipping knife and rapier from their sheaths.

"This is ridiculous," Meath complained. "If there's going to be a fight, I'd like to be able to *see* the enemy." He cupped a hand to his mouth and yelled, *"Come out, you yellow dogs! Show yourselves!"*

The words echoed in the granite canyons of the dead city.

"Well, that's given our position away very nicely," chided Shani. "If there *is* anybody out there, they'll have no trouble finding us now, will they?"

"Surely it's better to know what we're up against," Meath argued. "Then at least we can –"

"Ssshhhh!" Tycho was pressing a finger to his bristly lips.

They heard the grating of stone yet again.

Puzzled, Leandor scanned the area. "Where...?"

"There!" Shani pointed. "I'm certain it came from near the statues."

"Come on, you two, and be careful," Leandor warned. "Tycho, watch our backs."

The trio went toward the sculptures, fanning out, wary of surprises. Leandor approached from the front, Shani and Meath on opposite sides. But it took only a moment to realize nobody was hiding among the stone figures.

"Are you *sure* it came from over here, Shani?"

Meath called.

"Positive!"

Leandor stood next to the life-sized statue of a warrior mounted on a low pedestal. The warrior wore a breastplate and round helmet. He clutched a two-handed broadsword. As Leandor was about to turn away, a small quantity of fine grey dust fell from its chest.

"Dalveen?" Shani was beside him. "What are you looking at?"

"I'm not sure. Hold this, will you?" He gave her his sword, then reached up and touched the statue. The cool stone felt solid.

Meath arrived as a further tiny shower of dust fell, this time from the warrior's elbow joint.

"What is it, Leandor?" he said.

"I don't know. The thing seems to be decaying in front of us."

"Look!" Meath pointed to another statue. Dust was falling from it, too. "Perhaps it's the first tremors of an earthquake!"

"Then why isn't anything else affected?"

"It's no earthquake," Shani decided. "I think it's something less ... natural."

The sound of scraping stone rang out again. And this time there was no doubt of its source.

"It's coming from the *statues*!" she cried.

What happened then rooted the trio with amazement.

The warrior sculpture moved.

Its helmeted head turned jerkily sideways and down, as if to look at them. The heavy broadsword lifted, dislodging minute stone flakes in a puff of dust.

Leandor regained his stunned senses. *"Get back!"* he yelled. "Shani, my sword!" She tossed the weapon to him.

As they edged away, more statues began showing signs of life. Arms and legs wrenched free from the positions they had held for centuries. Craggy heads slowly twisted in new directions. And the screech of protesting granite marked every movement.

A splintering crack sounded. The warrior that had first moved yanked up one leg after the other, leaving the outline of its footprints on the pedestal. Then it stepped to the ground with a weighty thud. Around it, other figures were doing the same.

They started to lurch toward the astonished companions.

"Beware, Nightshade!" Tycho shouted from the rear. "This looks to be a truly powerful enchantment!"

"Let's see how they fare against a taste of steel," Leandor said.

He dashed to meet the foremost statue. A great swing from his blade connected with the rock-hard chest. But it did no more than loosen a few chippings, and the jarring impact almost parted Leandor from his sword. Cursing, he dodged out of the lumbering horror's path.

Dagger raised, a sculpture of a man in civilian garb lurched at Shani. She threw a knife at it. The blade broke in two on the carved folds of its robe.

"Damn!" she exclaimed, rapidly backing away.

Meath tried crossing his metal rapier with a stone blade. The statute he chose moved sluggishly, giving the mercenary a speed advantage, but his blows had no effect. He withdrew before it got any nearer.

The trio were back with Tycho now, watching helplessly as the small army of animated figures closed in.

"Have you noticed how their movements are becoming smoother?" Shani pointed out.

"Yes," Leandor agreed, "they seem to be getting faster."

"I believe the longer they are allowed their unnatural life, the more they will match human agility," Tycho told them. "At the moment they are hampered by the stiffness of ages-old immobility. It won't last. We have to defeat them quickly, Dalveen!"

"But *how*? Our weapons are useless against the things!"

"Sometimes the most prudent course is retreat."

"Yes, Leandor," Meath said. "Let's get out, and

at least give ourselves some thinking time."

"We'll try. But they're growing swifter by the minute. I'm not sure we can outpace them now."

He was right. They were still struggling across the rubble-covered square when the leading statues caught up.

"Scatter!" Leandor ordered. "Make for the horses!"

Tycho and Meath ran to the left, hugging the line of buildings. A fearsome warrior statue, wielding a battleaxe, started after them. They came to a stretch of free-standing wall, several times Meath's height, with a doorway in it. The remains of a large fallen tree could be seen on the other side.

"I have an idea," Tycho announced. "In here."

Meath glanced back and saw the statue getting closer. "It had better be good," he muttered, following him through the door frame.

Tycho began shoving at the tree trunk. "Help me block the entrance with this," he instructed.

Two ordinary men could not have managed it. But Meath's efforts and the homunculus's superior strength were enough to roll the dead wood in the door's direction.

They got it in place just as their pursuer arrived on the other side. The trunk didn't quite reach the top of the frame, leaving a gap through which the statue's head and shoulders were visible. It regarded the barrier with impassive eyes for a few seconds before pushing at it. Tycho and Meath leaned against the trunk on their side. After a brief struggle, the statue gave up.

Then it went back a few paces and started chopping at the wood with its double-headed axe.

"What now?" Meath said.

"This!" Tycho moved to the wall beside the door and placed his shoulder against it. "Hurry! Do the same!"

The mercenary went to the other side of the frame and added his force. "It seems too solid!" he called.

"Keep pushing!"

Relentlessly, the warrior's stone axe continued to cleave at the tree trunk. Already it was nearly halfway through.

"We're not going to shift this," Meath grunted.

"It's old and unstable. Use all your might!"

The wall swayed slightly. Small bits of stone rained down. Flaws opened in the masonry.

Intent only on reaching its quarry, the statue carried on oblivious, hacking without pause at the wooden obstruction.

"One more heave!" urged Meath, his muscles straining.

They felt the wall shudder. It tilted away from them at a crazy angle. Then gravity took over and it started to fall with a deep rumble.

The axeman statue looked up. There was no expression on its rigid face, but it took a couple of clumsy steps backward.

With a tremendous crash the wall collapsed.

Tons of stone engulfed the statue, simultaneously crushing and burying it.

A great cloud of choking dust obscured the scene for a moment. As it cleared, Tycho and Meath scrambled over the debris. Apart from the jagged stump of one of its arms, poking out of the fragments, there was no sign of the warrior.

"That was smart, Tycho," Meath congratulated him as they ran toward the horses. "Stone on stone, like fighting fire with fire!"

"Thank you."

"But I thought you weren't able to harm other life-forms."

"I cannot harm *human* life. And these creatures certainly aren't that." He glanced over his broad shoulder. Several more statues were in pursuit. "Nor was that the last of them, I'm afraid. Come, we must not linger!"

Leandor and Shani had run to the right. They slowed down to look when the wall collapsed, and saw Meath and Tycho being chased across the square.

"Watch out!" Shani warned.

The pause had allowed two statues to draw level with them. One, carrying a spear, went for Leandor.

The other, armed with sword and triangular-shaped shield, thundered at Shani. She fled.

Dodging a thrust from the lance, Leandor struck out, knowing it would be useless. The blade bounced off without causing the slightest damage. All he could do was parry the lance and hope to stay clear of his foe.

Then he noticed something. There were hairline cracks where the statue's spear arm and shoulder came together. He decided to concentrate on that area.

Swiftly he rushed in and swiped at the shoulder, landing a heavy blow. He swung again and hit the same spot. The statue lunged with its spear and Leandor had to swerve to avoid it. He managed a third blow and saw the cracks widen. As he prepared to deliver another strike the spearman jabbed at him. The lance tip missed his head by a whisker. But it gave him an opening. Leandor brought his sword down on the shoulder joint with as much force as he could muster.

His blade completely severed the arm. It fell to the ground, still clutching the spear. The mutilated sculpture, thrown off-balance, lurched into a wall.

It briefly crossed Leandor's mind that there was a certain irony in a one-armed man fighting a one-armed statue. The thought was quickly forgotten when he saw the diversion gave him an opportunity to get away.

He looked around for Shani.

She was running along the side of the square, the sword-wielding figure at her heels. It was boxing her in. A corner lay ahead where two buildings met. The entrance to the first was blocked. She made for the second, a semi-ruined structure with an exposed staircase. Scrabbling up a pile of rubble, Shani got herself on to the stairs, the statue close behind.

To her horror, she saw that the staircase ended one flight above, with a rickety landing projecting into empty air. There was no choice but to climb to it. The stairs rocked ominously under the weight of the statue trudging after her.

At the top, where the staircase connected to a brick wall, a long iron bar extended outward. She ducked under it to reach the landing. And had nowhere else to go.

The statue lumbered up the steps, its sword raised.

When its head reached the same level as her feet, she realized there was only one option. She backed across the landing cautiously, expecting the whole thing to give way at any moment. Then, as the upper part of the statue appeared, she ran toward the stairs and leapt at the bar with arms outstretched.

Her hands clasped the rusty metal. The rest of her body, carried on by momentum, continued to swing forward. She kept her legs straight, and the heel of her boots smashed into the statue's chest. By luck, she connected high, and with enough force to upset its centre of gravity.

The statue tottered for an instant, then pitched over the side. It plunged to the floor below and shattered into a hundred pieces.

Shani gulped a breath to steady herself and made her way down again.

Leandor was waiting at the bottom of the stairs. "Good thinking!" he told her. "Are you hurt?"

"Apart from stinging feet, no. Let's get going."

Outside, Tycho was trying to untether the horses while Meath fended off a hulking warrior statue. Shani and Dalveen hurried their way.

"Help with the mounts," Leandor said, heading for the mercenary.

Shani and the homunculus got the horses untied, and she took their reins.

Leandor joined Meath to combat the statue.

"Good to see you!" Meath declared. "A rapier's not much use for this kind of work!"

"Keep harrying it!" Leandor told him, swinging his broadsword. "And look for any cracks! They indicate a weakness!"

"Like around this one's neck?"

"Perfect!"

Leandor smashed his blade into the side of the statue's neck, gouging a lump out of it. The warrior backed away but kept fighting as Meath repeatedly worried at it with his sword. Leandor gave the neck a second hefty whack. More chips flew.

The retreating statue blundered into Shani. Before she could get out of its way, it back-handed her with its free arm. She went down, letting go of the reins. The horses shied in panic and galloped off.

"*Damnation!*" she spat.

Tycho hurtled into the statue's side with enormous impact. The warrior staggered and fell. Leandor closed in, lifted his sword and brought it down on the neck. Two more blows hacked off the head. It rolled a short distance and lay staring at them.

The decapitated warrior awkwardly attempted to get up. They ignored it.

"We'll never catch the horses now," Meath said. "And here come more of the blasted things!"

Over a dozen statues were approaching from different directions.

"We'll just have to try outrunning them," Leandor decided. "Follow me!"

They began jogging toward the street that led to the river.

CHAPTER 17

"They're gaining on us!" Meath yelled.

"This way!" Leandor made for a narrow road leading out of the square. It rose toward the hill they had stood upon earlier, and beyond that lay the river.

Fracturing the silence with the pounding of heavy footfalls, the group of hexed statues kept coming.

The road grew steeper. And no more than a hundred paces on, it disappeared into dense undergrowth. Shani, Meath and Leandor were tiring. Tycho, like the pack of undead figures behind, showed no sign of exhaustion.

"We'll never penetrate this jungle!" Shani panted as they reached the tangled vegetation.

"Use your blades!" Leandor barked.

They plunged in, hacking wildly. Creeping vines snagged their ankles, prickles stung exposed flesh, palms lashed at their faces. Unseen at the rear, their stone hunters powered through the greenery as though it didn't exist.

Bleeding from cuts and scratches, the quartet finally emerged in open ground on the hillside. They waded into the knee-high grass and began climbing. The statues crashed out of the bushes and followed.

Leandor arrived at the top first, fighting for breath, and looked down the other side. The incline swept to a dense wood, and a scattering of ruins could be seen among the trees. Further on, a patch of water reflected the sunlight.

As they started to descend, Shani said, "If we don't shake them off before the river there'll be nowhere left to run, Dalveen."

"I know. We'll try losing them in the trees."

"I would not be too hopeful of doing so," Tycho cautioned as he glanced back at the macabre figures. "They were obviously created for the sole purpose of destroying anyone in search of the book. These creatures are mindless killers!"

The unstoppable statues lumbered after them into the wood.

"Keep going!" Leandor urged the others past him, pointing the way with his sword before bringing up the rear. Meath took the lead.

Having to weave around overgrown ruins slowed them, and the deadly sculptures were closing the gap. Before long, the river came into view, and the path Meath chose narrowed between thickets of trees, forcing them to run single-file. Then a round tower appeared ahead. While the others skirted it, Leandor turned and saw the statues catching up.

He decided to try buying his companions some time.

Sword raised, he faced the leading figure. Careful to stay out of range of its probing spear, he unleashed a series of defensive slashes. Other statues quickly arrived, driving him back against the moss-covered masonry. One managed to slip by him, cutting off his escape route.

Edging around the curve of the tower, frantically parrying thrusts from daggers, swords and lances, he came to the entrance. The only option was to duck inside. From what he could see of the dark, cool interior, the hollow structure seemed basically sound. But there was no other door, just an open staircase that wound to the roof. Assuming the roof still existed.

The statues were streaming in after him. All he could do was take the stairs. Relentlessly, the stone figures thundered in his wake.

Although there was a gleam of light somewhere

above, he was climbing in almost complete darkness. Fearful of decaying steps, he kept close to the outside wall. Several times he scraped painfully against the rotting brickwork.

A statue got near enough to swipe at his legs. He spun, raining blows down on the creature, battering at its shield. A lucky stroke cut into its face. Already close to the stairs' edge, the stone warrior stumbled over the side and pitched headlong to the ground. Leandor was moving again when the shattering impact rang out.

Another two turns of the spiral staircase brought him to a short passage that led to a doorway. Dashing through, he found himself on a large flat roof with a low battlement all the way around. It was complete except for one area, directly ahead, where a chunk was missing. He ran to the break and looked down. Far below, the river flowed by the tower's base.

The statues poured from the opening behind him and approached grimly.

He was trapped.

Meath, Shani and Tycho burst out of the scrub and on to the riverbank a little way upstream from the tower.

"Where's Dalveen?" Shani said.

Tycho looked back. "I thought he was following us."

"And what happened to those wretched statues?" Meath added, surveying the treeline.

"Oh, gods," Shani whispered. "You don't think...?"

"Look! Up there!" Tycho pointed to the top of the tower.

Leandor's head and shoulders could just be seen. He was backing to the edge. As they watched, several stone figures came into view.

"Stay here, Tycho!" she yelled. "Come on, Meath!"

They ran back into the wood, leaving the homunculus anxiously gazing at the drama above.

Minutes later they were at the tower. On entering, they saw the smashed statue that had fallen. They raced to the stairs and pounded up them.

Leandor knew he couldn't hope to fight off the slowly advancing monstrosities. Nor was there any way to escape.

He was as good as dead.

But there was one thing left to try. He remembered Tycho's comment about the statues being mindless, created for the single purpose of tracking and slaughtering anyone looking for the book. Leandor decided to test the theory.

The fact that it would probably kill him didn't make a lot of difference under the circumstances.

He slipped his sword into the scabbard on his

back and began walking toward the enemy. They moved forward, ready to butcher him. When he got as near as he dared, he stopped.

Then suddenly turned and ran for the battlement.

They stampeded after him, waving swords and spears, his destruction their only aim.

He took a deep breath as he reached the broken wall.

And jumped.

Shani and Meath dashed on to the roof just as the statues leapt after him.

"*Dalveen!*" Shani screamed.

Leandor's one-armed, black garbed figure hurtled from the tower and plunged down to the river. He was instantly followed by the band of grey stone pursuers, falling like so many dead weights, bodies rigid.

Princess Bethan gasped in horror, hands to her mouth.

Avoch-Dar killed the image with a swift gesture. The crystal returned to displaying a kaleidoscope of swirling colours.

"It's a trick," she said, tears coursing down her cheeks.

"Oh no, my dear. What you have just seen is real enough."

"Why show me something so horrible?"

"To give you pain, of course. And to demonstrate

that your precious Nightshade has more to think about than coming to your aid."

She gave way to despair.

The sorcerer smiled wickedly. Everything was going to plan.

Leandor hit the river.

He managed to straighten as he fell and knifed into the water cleanly. Even so, the impact was tremendous, and he nearly let out the breath he held.

Dropping from such a height meant he was deep before his momentum slowed. His hand struck mud and was buried to the elbow. As he pulled loose, a bulky grey object plummeted down beside him, throwing up a murky cloud. Another followed, missing his head by inches, and was embedded in the silt.

The statues were sinking all around. If one landed on top of him, he was finished. He kicked with his legs, pushing himself further out into the river.

His lungs were bursting. And with only one arm, he didn't think he could make the surface.

Meath and Shani got to the edge of the tower as the last of the statues slammed into the water below. They saw Tycho hurrying across the bank.

"How can he swim with one arm, Meath?" Shani cried. "He'll drown down there!"

"If the fall hasn't already done for him," the mercenary replied. "Here, take this!" He shoved his sword into her hand.

"What are you –?"

"Give me room!"

She moved aside as Meath retreated a couple of steps.

Then he ran forward and dived off the roof.

Chapter 18

Leandor was drowning.

No matter how hard he tried to reach it, the surface never seemed closer. His limbs ached, his chest burnt with the need for air, his vision blurred.

He started to black out.

It would be so easy to let go, to stop struggling and allow the cool water to fill his lungs. So simple to drift down to the muddy depths and rest. To surrender to eternal sleep.

No.

His mind rebelled and pushed away the notion. Having come this far, and with so many depending on him, he would rather be damned for ever than give up now. The river would not take him without a fight.

He gathered every scrap of remaining strength and willed his exhausted body toward the light above. It was a last supreme effort. There was no second chance if he failed.

The surface was near. Near enough, he was sure, that his outstretched fingers would pierce it at any second. But it mocked him. The world of life-giving air beyond was an illusion he couldn't get to.

He began to sink again.

Then there was a surge of displaced water as something plunged in next to him. He was aware of a flurry of movement, of thrashing arms and legs, and an impression of flowing red hair.

A firm hand grasped the back of his shirt. He felt a jolt as powerful legs kicked downward. Leandor began rising, pulled by the scruff of his neck, and he found energy to kick too, hastening the ascent. The infinity of space that had imprisoned him became mere distance, a journey completed in the span of three heartbeats.

His head broke the surface. He took a great gulp of fresh, clean air, instantly relieving the explosive pressure in his lungs. Meath bobbed up beside him, panting for breath himself, and pushed him to the bank. Splashing out to them, Tycho helped drag Leandor to dry land.

He lay wheezing and gasping, inhaling draughts of precious oxygen between watery coughs.

Meath and Tycho looked down at him. Almost immediately, Shani appeared, making a trio of concerned faces.

"Are you all right, Dalveen?" she asked anxiously.

He was too winded to do more than nod.

She turned to the others. "Do you know if he swallowed a lot of water? Should we try pumping him out?"

Leandor cleared his throat and managed to say, "No. I'm ... all ... right. Didn't swallow ... any." He coughed a little more and began sitting up.

"Steady," Meath cautioned, placing a supportive hand on his shoulder. "Don't overdo it."

"I'm ... fine. And I owe ... you ... my thanks. I'm in ... your debt."

"Forget it." The mercenary smiled. "It's what comrades are for. I know you'd do the same for me."

"Nevertheless, I'm ... grateful." His head was clearing and his strength returning. "And thanks for ... your help, Tycho."

"Think nothing of it."

Shani glanced at the river. "It's a good thing those statues were even worse swimmers than you, Dalveen. Do you think we've seen the last of them?"

"Probably. Apart from the few we wrecked in the city, I'm sure they all came after me."

"What do we do now?" Meath said.

"First we build a fire and get you two dry," Shani announced. "Then we'll look for the horses."

"We'll be lucky to catch them," the mercenary sighed.

"Oh, and let's try finding something to sharpen our blades with," she added. "Hacking at stone is certain to have blunted them."

"And after that?" Meath persisted. "Shouldn't we search that place for the book?" He jabbed a thumb in the city's direction.

"A quick ... inspection of the major buildings," Leandor suggested. "But I'm more convinced than ever that ... what we seek ... isn't there."

"Still relying on your instinct?" Shani said.

"Partly. But mostly it's for the reasons I gave in the library. First, it doesn't seem a logical place to leave something as valuable as the book. It's obviously not even a demon city, remember. Second, Melva said we'd know the location when we came to it, and we've seen nothing to indicate that."

Meath wasn't happy. "We *might*, if we examine the city thoroughly enough."

"It's possible. But I'd say we weren't at the end of our quest yet. My vote is to continue eastward."

"Without horses?" Meath asked.

"We may have no choice."

That gave them all something to think about while gathering firewood.

"I've never seen a landscape change so suddenly," Shani remarked as she surveyed the desolate terrain ahead.

"Nor grow quite so hot this quickly," Meath complained, wiping perspiration from his brow. "Too much water yesterday and not enough today, eh, Leandor?"

"We do seem to have gone from one extreme to the other. Maybe we shouldn't have left the river."

"I think it was the right decision," Tycho said. "Following the river's twists and bends was too time consuming. At least we are now heading true east."

"Yes, and on *foot*," Meath grumbled. "I still say we should have built a raft."

"And ended up where?" Shani responded. "If the prophecy said east, then east is the way we have to go."

They fell into despondent silence.

Their search of the city had revealed nothing. No book, and no horses. Which also meant no food or water, as their mounts had carried off the saddlebags and canteens. All they could do was walk, and since parting company with the river, the land was rapidly becoming desert.

"It's not too late to turn back and build that raft," Meath repeated. "We've only been walking for a day and a half."

"Feels like a week," Shani said.

"We made a decision yesterday and I'm sticking with it," Leandor stated. "But you aren't obliged to. I'll understand if anybody wants to go back. After all, none of you originally intended joining this quest."

"Speaking for myself, I may not have asked to come along, but now I wouldn't have it any other way," Shani told him. "Let's keep going."

"That's how I see it too, Dalveen," Tycho added.

"Of course I agree," Meath said. "It's just all this slogging in the heat that's getting me down."

"None of us like it," Leandor replied. "But I have the same feeling today I had yesterday, when I thought I was going to drown. It seemed so futile to give up after coming this far. I'm resolved to see this quest to its end, and if that means dying in the process, so be it. Naturally I don't expect the same sacrifice from anyone else."

"I'll make my own decisions about whether I put my life at risk, thank you," Shani flared. "And I decided some time ago to see this thing through, no matter what the outcome. I think that goes for all of us, doesn't it?"

Tycho and Meath nodded.

Leandor smiled at each of them in turn. "Thank

you. I couldn't wish for better companions."

"Don't spoil it by getting sloppy," Shani warned him.

"Er, excuse me," Tycho interrupted, "but what do you think that might be?" He pointed to the horizon.

They shielded their eyes and squinted. The sunlight flashed on something green and shiny in the distance.

"It's a way off," Leandor decided, "and if it's a building of some kind, pretty big."

"Let's go and find out," Meath suggested.

Princess Bethan tried to conceal the shock she felt.

"You want me to do what?*" she gasped.*

"Putting it that way makes it sound as though you have a choice," the sorcerer told her, "which of course you haven't. It is really quite simple, my dear. Tomorrow afternoon, you and I will be married."

"Haven't you done enough to humiliate me?"

"If I were a less tolerant man, I might be offended by that remark. Surely you would not spurn the chance to wed Delgarvo's new ruler? To sit at his right hand as he goes on to conquer the rest of the world? Many women would be eager for such an opportunity?"

"Marry one of them then!"

"Ah, but they are not princesses of the realm, my child. They do not occupy a position of importance as you do."

"What's the point of it, Avoch-Dar? What do you hope to achieve with this farce?"

"The marriage will make me the undisputed head of Delgarvo's royal family. It will help consolidate my position, and give me authority in the eyes of the people."

"Don't depend on it. My father's subjects are not so easily fooled."

"My desire is to establish a dynasty," he continued, ignoring her. "King Avoch-Dar has a certain ring to it, don't you think?"

"You're insane! You must be, to believe I don't know what would happen to me once I've served my purpose! I would rather face death now than endure this mockery and die later at your whim!"

"Come now, Bethan, it won't be that *bad." A wicked smile twisted his lips. "After all, it's not as though anyone else is likely to claim your hand."*

"That's it, isn't it? You're doing this to punish Dalveen, aren't you?"

"I confess that does add a certain satisfaction to the plan. But don't look so glum, my intended; I'm sure if the noble Nightshade was here, he would give his right arm to... Oh, how silly of me. He's already done that, hasn't he?" The magician burst into scornful laughter.

"You swine!" she screamed. "You spawn of a swamp lizard! You –"

"Take her away!" he snapped.

Two guards rushed forward and bundled Bethan to the council chamber's doors.

"Till the morrow, beloved!" he called as they dragged the cursing Princess out of earshot.

Avoch-Dar went to his magic crystal. With a swift movement of his hands he conjured a vision of Leandor and the others. He watched as they approached the odd structure in the heart of the barren waste.

"Fascinating," he whispered. "Quite fascinating."

It was a huge pyramid made of green glass. Or something that looked like glass.

Shani ran her hand across the smooth surface. "It's *cold*, despite the sun. What kind of material is it?"

"I don't know," Leandor said, "I've never seen the like."

"Have you noticed there are no seams?" Meath pointed out. "The entire thing appears to have been fashioned from a single titanic piece of ... whatever it is."

"There is no one in our present age with the skill to construct this," Tycho decided.

Scrubby grass and parched earth had given way to sand before they reached the pyramid. Drifted by wind, it had formed small yellow mounds along the structure's base. Tycho noticed something growing out of one of them and beckoned the others over.

"Does anyone recognize this plant?" he asked.

The slender stem bore purple, bell-shaped flowers containing clusters of tiny black berries.

"I do," Shani said. "We call it dwale where I come from."

"Or belladonna," Meath added. "Those berries are poisonous."

"Precisely," Tycho confirmed. "I have no doubt you are familiar with it under its most common name, Dalveen. Nightshade. *Deadly* nightshade. Your namesake."

"Yes," Leandor replied thoughtfully. "As a matter of fact it appears on the coat of arms Eldrick presented me with."

"Look." Shani pointed further along the shiny base. "More of them. How do they live in these conditions?"

"Like everything else in this land," Meath said, "they defy the usual laws of Nature. But the real significance is finding them here at all. I see no plants of any other kind. It's too much of a coincidence."

"It could well be a sign," Tycho speculated.

They walked to the corner and turned it. In common with the side they had just examined, nothing broke the shiny façade. But in the centre of the third and final face they came upon an enormous door. Clumps of nightshade grew on either side.

The door was set flush into the green surround and made of burnished bronze. There was no handle, keyhole or any other obvious means of gaining entrance. Engraved on it was a large five-pointed star, each point touching the circle it was surrounded by.

"A pentagram," Tycho stated. But he had no need to identify it. They all knew the ancient symbol and its ages-old association with black magic.

Meath gave the door a shove. "The next question is how we're going to get in."

"Logically, as the door has the same angle as the wall, it's unlikely to swing inward or outward," Tycho reasoned. "It would probably slide to one side or raise up."

There were no gaps on the outside edges, so they began clearing sand from the bottom.

"It looks as though it *does* go up," Meath said, "and there might be just enough of a crack here to give us purchase. Lend your strength, Tycho."

Leandor and Shani watched as the homunculus and the soldier of fortune worked their fingers into the cleft. They heaved and strained, but the door wouldn't lift.

"Help us, you two," Meath panted.

Shani knelt beside him and joined the struggle. As Leandor went forward to do likewise the palm of his hand brushed against the pentagram.

The instant he touched the door it started to rise.

Despite weighing what must have been many tons, it lifted smoothly and without sound.

Meath, Tycho and Shani, on their knees, gaped in amazement as the mighty portal opened wide.

"That was no mere chance," Shani declared. "It moved for *you*, Dalveen!"

Leandor said nothing. He stared into the interior. It was light.

"How can it be lit?" Meath wanted to know. "There are no windows, lanterns or torches that I can see."

"Perhaps it's occupied," Shani said. The thought made her shudder.

"I don't think so," Leandor guessed. "Look at the amount of undisturbed dust there is on the floor." He stepped through the entrance and his boots sank into a thick carpet of grime. A long, wide corridor ran straight ahead.

Tycho came after him and gazed around. "The interior seems to be made from the same material as the outside, except it's grey instead of green. And the builders had the means to create something like glass that is not only extremely tough but also allows light to enter."

"Yet it isn't transparent."

"Exactly. It is, so to speak, one-way glass. If the demon race was responsible for this, they had some remarkable secrets, Dalveen."

"There's the top of a staircase at the far end," Meath said.

They walked to it and climbed down the broad steps to an arched doorway. Beyond was a narrow passage from which other corridors went off in various directions at acute angles. A quick inspection showed that each of these led to further passages that branched in turn.

"It's a maze," Leandor decided.

"Perhaps one of us should stay here to guard the exit," Meath suggested.

"I think it would be a better idea if you all stayed," Leandor said.

"*What?*" Shani exclaimed. "There could be anything in there!"

"Yes, there could. And I have to face it by myself. I've endangered your lives enough already."

"You could wander in this place for an eternity and never find your way out," Meath warned.

Shani took off her headband and picked at it. "This might help. It's a continuous thread of material. Attach one end to your belt and we'll hold on to the other."

Leandor smiled. "That's a brilliant idea. But the maze may be longer than the thread. What then?"

"Then we'll find something else to tie to it. We could unravel Meath's shirt, for instance."

The mercenary scowled. "Yes, I suppose so, if

necessary. However, I think going in alone is most unwise. Won't you let one of us come with you?"

"No. Let's not argue about it. Please." He tied the thread in place. "And I don't want anybody to think of following me. If I'm not back by ... let's say dawn, try to make your way home."

"For what it's worth," Tycho said, "mazes are said to have originated with the demon race, and the ones we have today are supposed to be a survival of a fragment of their knowledge. If that's true, this one may be built on the classic pattern. That means taking left turns to reach its centre, right turns to get out again."

"That seems as good a plan as any. Where did you pick up such an obscure piece of information?"

"I heard Avoch-Dar talking about it once."

A look of grim determination came to Leandor's face. "Thank you for reminding me why we're here, Tycho."

He entered the labyrinth.

Chapter 19

Leandor heeded Tycho's advice and took only left turns.

Several passageways came to dead ends. When that happened he retraced his steps and moved on to the next left-forking corridor. Once, he managed to walk in a complete circle, and wouldn't have known except for the trailing thread. After that he was especially careful not to let it break.

Walls, floor and ceiling were made of the same shiny, grey material wherever he went. Nor did the light vary. He soon lost all sense of how far into the maze he had travelled, and his ability to judge time also began to desert him. So he could not tell when he first noticed the floor starting to slope.

The path he followed was leading him downwards.

Eventually he came to a passage that levelled and ran to a door. It was normal size, but in every other way identical to the one above, with a smaller pentagram etched on its bronze surface.

He hesitated, aware of the absolute silence, and wondered what might be on the other side. Finally, as before, he placed his palm against the magic symbol.

The door rose.

And there was no doubt he had arrived at the heart of the labyrinth.

Before him was a huge circular chamber. It had a domed ceiling, much higher than the ceiling in the maze. There was another door, twin to the one he had just entered, directly opposite. No kind of decoration relieved the smooth greyness.

A plinth stood in the exact centre of the room. Leandor estimated its height to be roughly equal to his chest. The rectangular, flat-topped slab was black, but looked to have been fashioned from the same polished substance as everything else.

Upon it lay the Book of Shadows.

His heart beat so loud and fast he was sure anyone else present would have heard it.

He undid the thread from his belt, dropped it, and cautiously advanced.

The book was large. It compared in length to the

span between his elbow and fingertips. Its width was perhaps half that. His clenched fist would just about match its thickness. The yellow-brown binding resembled tanned hide. From the spine a pair of metal hinges extended a quarter of the way across the cover. There was no title or ornamentation.

It did not seem fragile or decayed, yet somehow gave the impression of being old beyond all reckoning.

Leandor was conscious of a deeper feeling, too, one he would never find words to describe. He sensed what he could only think of as an invisible pulse of energy coming from the book. And although he did not understand how, he knew the aura of power was directed by a form of intelligence. An intelligence unlike anything he had ever encountered before.

It was as though he was in the presence of something that ... *lived.*

He reached out to touch it.

Then a shadow, cast from behind, fell across him and the volume.

He turned to face its source.

Shani cut away Meath's other shirtsleeve. The first, unravelled and tied to the last of the fibre from her headband, was almost exhausted.

Tycho had been playing out the yarn as Leandor

penetrated deeper into the maze. "We may not need more thread after all," he reported. "Dalveen hasn't drawn on it for several minutes now."

"Let's hope that means he's arrived at the centre," Meath said, "rather than been stopped by something."

"I regret not arguing with his decision to go in alone," Shani complained. "He might need help in there."

"Do not underestimate his abilities," Tycho reminded her.

Meath sat on the floor, back against the wall, his intertwined hands around a raised knee. "Nevertheless, we should give some thought to what we're going to do if he doesn't make it."

Shani glared at him. "You can be cold-hearted at times, Meath."

"No, merely practical. Should Leandor fail, and lose his life, what would you have us do then? Turn and walk away from the book? Abandon the chance of gaining it when we're so near?"

"But one reason Dalveen set out to find the book was because it might bring back his arm. If he … died, why would *we* need it?"

"You're not thinking, girl. As you said, that's one reason. The other is that it contains knowledge. And demon knowledge obviously means great power. We might be able to use that power against Avoch-Dar."

"It's a good point," Tycho added. "Assuming it's here, the book may prove a valuable weapon."

"And you think we could succeed in recovering it where Dalveen failed?" Shani asked, a mocking tone in her voice.

"Perhaps," Meath replied evenly. "I suggest that if Leandor hasn't returned by dawn we go in rather than do as he said and leave."

"Then we're of one mind," she said, "because I'd decided to do that anyway. Not for the damned book, but to see if I can aid him. Or to avenge his death."

The first think Leandor took in was the size of the being he faced.

Twice the height and double the girth of a man, the creature seemed a crossbreed, part human, part nameless hell-spawn.

Golden armour adorned its massive trunk. Thick black hair covered its arms. Either hand could encircle Leandor's neck with room to spare. And easily crush it. The legs, swathed in matted fur, ended in hooves similar to those of a war-horse.

Unlike the body, the head was hairless, the skin having the quality of pale, worn leather. The large ears were spiked and elf-like. Dark bushy eyebrows arched above saucer eyes, their black irises and white surrounds flecked with pinpricks of crimson. The nose was a flattened upturned snout. A tusk jutted from either end of its gash of a mouth.

It held a sword of burnished steel which, stood upright, would have been taller than Leandor. So shiny was the blade it could serve as a mirror.

As the creature strode toward him, Leandor saw the tip of a forked tail swishing just above the polished floor. He noticed, too, that the chamber's other door was open, explaining where the being had come from.

Backing away from the plinth, Leandor drew his sword.

But the attack he expected did not begin. The giant stopped short and they stared at each other in silence for a moment.

Then the creature spoke.

"I am Kreid," it boomed. "Guardian of the Book."

"I am Dalveen Leandor, known also as Nightshade, and I have come to claim it."

Kreid's icy gaze did not waver. "Empires have risen and fallen, oceans dried up, mountains turned to dust while I endured my seclusion here, waiting for such a challenge. You are the first of your kind."

"And I will be the last."

"Will you? Only the prophesied Champion may claim as his right the chance to carry off the tome."

"I am he."

"The doors to this place bear an enchantment barring all but the predicted hero. You have entered, and that is in your favour. But even the strongest spells can grow weak given time. And more time has passed since they were cast than you could possibly imagine."

"I overcame the perils."

"Yes. But you have yet to best me, and I am not easily brushed aside."

"Are you a demon?"

"No. I was *created* by those you call demons. Some of their blood runs in my veins."

"What happened to them?"

"They went ... somewhere else."

"Where?"

"As far as the most distant star, as near as your next thought. You would not understand."

"Why did they go?"

"This world could contain them no longer. And the coming of your race, like a pestilence, sealed their decision to move on."

"Leaving you behind."

"The book is more precious to me than my own life. My sole purpose was to stay and defend it."

"Now I am here to take it, by right."

"No, little man. I say again, you have won only the *chance* to acquire this prize."

"Have I not proved myself?"

"Not against me. I may wish you to be the long-awaited one, and have done with my ordeal of endless guardianship, but I have no choice in the matter. I must assume you are a mere interloper and do my best to kill you."

"I seek the book in order to do battle with an evil tyrant, a black sorcerer who would banish good from this world. Does such a cause not move your heart?"

"Your petty affairs are no concern of mine. And the book's awesome power is not something I would lightly bestow, even if I could. You must *take* it. If you can." He lifted his mighty sword. "Do not waste your breath on words, Nightshade. Save it for combat!"

The Guardian moved forward.

Kreid thundered in for the attack.

Leandor swiftly backed away, his blade raised defensively. He knew that until he had the Guardian's measure it was fatal to be in range of his gigantic sword. The best plan was to stay clear and try to spot his weak points.

The thought came easier than the deed.

Kreid displayed an agility Leandor would not have believed possible in one of such tremendous size. As to weaknesses, he feared the Guardian had none. If that was so, he faced the most dangerous kind of opponent; both immensely strong and fast-moving.

Leandor couldn't find a way through the rain of

deadly blows directed at him. It was a continuous retreat rather than a duel. And it was already beginning to look as though he would be exhausted long before the Guardian spent his abundant energy.

The game of cat and mouse could not last for ever. Leandor had to go on the offensive.

Kreid was using his blade like a scythe, sweeping it before him left to right, right to left as he advanced. Getting in its path meant being cut in two. But there was a point of stillness when the sword reached the limit of its arc before slicing back again. In that tiny fraction of a second the Guardian was exposed. Trying to exploit the opening was a tremendous risk.

Leandor decided to take it.

He edged forward, letting several swipes pass as near as he dared. The great broadsword, which he would probably have had trouble lifting even with two arms, whistled as it cleaved the air.

Then the breach came and he darted in.

His blade cracked against Kreid's armour fruitlessly, but the unexpected move was enough to break the rhythm of his swings. Leandor seized the opportunity to strike once more. This time he aimed lower, cutting deep into his foe's shaggy thigh. The Guardian grunted with pain, faltered briefly, and renewed his assault with added fury.

Leandor threw himself aside, breath laboured, a sheen of sweat dappling his brow.

He noticed that the wound he inflicted was weeping, not the scarlet of human blood, but black, gummy fluid like tar. The sight encouraged him. Perhaps this being was not as invulnerable as he thought.

Now Leandor followed a basic rule of one-to-one combat: if you injure your opponent, try to do it again as quickly as possible.

Dodging under the speeding sword, he side-stepped, spun and arrived at the Guardian's back. As he hoped, the armoured breastplate was designed to protect only its wearer's chest. At the rear a gap extended from waist to neck where the armour didn't meet, criss-crossed with leather bindings that held it in place. He slashed downward into this unprotected area. His blade severed the bindings and laid open the flesh beneath.

Kreid bellowed.

And swung around so suddenly Leandor very nearly caught the full force of his sword.

As it was, the point ripped through his shirt and raked his chest, gashing a bloody scar. It felt like a hot brand had been run over his skin. A step nearer and the stroke would have carved his innards.

He gasped and fell back, expecting a follow-up blow to finish him.

But Kreid was entangled with the armour,

which had begun to slip from his body when the bindings were cut. He tore himself free and hurled it aside. It clattered noisily on the gleaming floor.

Leandor used the diversion to scramble away. The Guardian came after him, his face twisted in murderous resolve. Another deluge of scathing passes drove Leandor further back, towards the wall. Despite his wounds, Kreid showed no sign of slowing, no loss of determination to slaughter the outsider. If anything, his attack was more frenzied.

The Guardian unleashed a swing meant to part Leandor's head from his body. He ducked and the blade hammered into the wall, hewing out a sizeable chunk of the tough, grey material.

A frantic dash took Leandor to the centre of the chamber, within a few paces of the book's resting place. Kreid was close behind. Convinced that running was futile, Leandor turned, sweeping his blade at the Guardian. The slash was parried by the edge of Kreid's sword. As was the next, and the next. Then their blades met with a crash that sent Leandor's flying from his hand.

He stood unarmed before the triumphant creature.

Kreid moved in for the kill.

Leandor swerved to avoid the first slash. A leap carried him clear of the second. But the tireless onslaught continued. Dodging and weaving as he retreated, he desperately sought respite from the Guardian's storm of fury.

He backed into something that blocked his escape. It could only have been the stand holding the book.

Kreid raised his sword high above his head.

"Your quest has ended, Nightshade," he hissed. *"Prepare to die!"*

He brought down the weapon in a final savage strike.

Finding a last reserve of strength, Leandor half rolled, half fell to one side.

He glimpsed Kreid's face. A look of naked terror flashed across it as he realized his razor-sharp blade would not meet flesh. Unstoppable, it plunged toward the very thing he was created to protect.

It struck the book.

"Is that all you can remember, Tycho?" Shani asked.

"Yes. Avoch-Dar took me so much for granted that he often spoke of many important things when I was present, but he never went into detail on that subject. He simply said his power was to be greatly increased, and soon. It stayed in my mind because he repeated it so often."

"Well, conquering Delgarvo *would* increase his power, that's for certain," Meath said. "Where's the mystery?"

"I do not think he meant military power," Tycho

replied, "and he openly discussed his plans for the invasion. No, this was something else. I believe he may have been referring to his *magical* powers."

"As if they weren't strong enough already," Shani remarked.

"All the more reason for us to get ourselves to the heart of this labyrinth," Meath argued. "Come to that, why wait until dawn? There's no time like the present."

"It would mean defying Dalveen's wish," Tycho reminded him.

The mercenary was about to say something when a blood-freezing cry echoed from the labyrinth. It was a primeval wail, a fusion of pain and anger, and they had not heard its like from man nor beast.

"What in Hades was *that*?" he exclaimed.

Shani leapt to her feet. "I don't care what we promised, we're going in!"

Meath snatched his sword. "Tycho, keep firm hold on that thread and guide us!"

They ran into the maze.

Kreid screamed again.

When his blade came down against the book it was as though he had hit an anvil. His sword had instantly shattered into a thousand fragments like crystals of ice. An uncontrollable spasm tore through him and he roared in agony.

Now Leandor lay awestruck as he watched the giant writhing in pain. The sticky black liquid the Guardian had for blood was welling from both his palms. It overflowed and splattered on to the floor. Jerking convulsions ran the length of his arms. His chest heaved. The mighty head snapped from side to side and more dark fluid gushed from his mouth.

Kreid clutched at his throat. A horrible gurgling sound replaced the tormented wailing. He swayed drunkenly.

Leandor shook off his trance and scrambled out of the way.

The Guardian staggered and fell. His massive body slammed to the ground with a bone-jarring impact. A single, awful, shudder rippled through him.

And he was still.

The newly returned silence was broken only by Leandor's heavy breathing.

At length he slowly got up, wincing at the sting from his chest wound. He cautiously approached Kreid and gently toed his body with a boot tip. There was no doubt that he was dead.

Leandor turned to the book. There wasn't a mark on it.

The cold hand of fear caressed his spine. This ancient object had killed its own protector. Perhaps it was to defend itself against Kreid's blade. It could equally be that any contact would prove fatal. In either case it seemed poor payment for the Guardian's aeons of devotion.

He stared at the tome and felt once more the invisible throb of dark power radiating from it. And he sensed that what he had just seen was a mere taste of that power.

But what would it do to *him*?

There was only one way to find out.

He reached for the book.

Avoch-Dar peered into the crystal anxiously, his fists clenched, a look of intense concentration furrowing his brow.

His retinue, scattered about Torpoint's Great Hall, watched in silence. The atmosphere was strained. None present dared so much as move.

The sorcerer had followed Leandor's progress through the maze beneath the glass pyramid. He had seen his encounter with Kreid, and the Guardian's death. Now he observed his old enemy standing in contemplation before the book.

At last Leandor extended his hand. Avoch-Dar leaned forward to savour the moment. Leandor's fingertips hesitated near the ancient tome's binding.

The image in the crystal quivered. It faded and blurred, then vanished altogether in a swirling blizzard of dense grey mist.

"Beelzebub's tail!" the wizard cried. "Not now!"

He made a conjuration to bring back the likeness, but to no avail.

"The power of the book has clouded my magic!" he raged. "The crystal is blind! Blind!"

Those assembled quaked at his towering rage. They steeled themselves to suffer his wrath.

It did not come. Their master's demeanour at once softened. He sank back into his throne and displayed and almost benign smile.

"But he has the book," the sorcerer muttered with something very much like satisfaction. "He has the book..."

Avoch-Dar's followers exchanged mystified glances.

He was still alive.

Leandor had placed his hand on the book and lived.

A sigh of relief escaped his lips.

He ran his fingers across the binding. It could have been his imagination, but he thought he felt a slight tingling sensation, and there was a vague impression of ... *warmth*. But nothing about the remarkable tome surprised him now. He had seen a demonstration of its power.

That didn't stop him shuddering.

When he lifted the cover he half expected the paper inside to be rotted, or at least brittle. It wasn't. It was just a little yellowed, like the binding.

The first page was blank. The second had a picture of a pentagram. The next was covered in incomprehensible lettering of a kind he had never seen before. The one after had more of the same, strewn with magical symbols. He didn't understand any of it, and wondered how he was going to use a book he couldn't read.

He resisted the temptation to turn further pages and closed it. The others were probably worried about him and he ought to be getting back. He looked around for his sword and saw it lying on the other side of Kreid's body.

Returning the blade to its scabbard, he glanced down at the Guardian. The creature's flesh was already beginning to decompose and give off the sickly odour of decay. Having waited countless centuries, it seemed death was impatient to claim its own.

Leandor went back to the book. Carrying something of that size presented problems for a man with only one arm, but he was sure he would manage. He just hoped it didn't mind being moved.

The thought made him smile. Grimly.

Laying his forearm across the cover, he clasped the book's spine and slipped it from the stand. Then he brought it against the side of his body, one end in his palm, the other under his armpit. Its weight didn't trouble him.

He spotted the thread near the entrance and

walked toward it. And stopped. Footsteps and muffled voices echoed from the corridor outside.

Leandor put the book back on its stand, stood in front of it and drew his sword.

Shani appeared in the doorway, Tycho and Meath close behind.

"Dalveen!" she exclaimed, rushing to him. "Thank the gods you're alive!"

He relaxed and replaced his blade.

"You're wounded," Shani said when she saw his tattered, bloodstained shirt.

"It's nothing. I was lucky."

"Who, or *what*, was that?" Meath asked, nodding at Kreid's corpse.

"The Guardian of the Book," Leandor replied. "His name was Kreid."

"You did well to overcome such a formidable opponent," Tycho said.

"I didn't. The book killed him." He took in their puzzled expressions and added, "I'll explain later."

Meath was intrigued. "The Book of Shadows? You have it?"

Leandor stepped aside to let them see the volume. They cautiously advanced and stared at it.

"I don't like it," Shani declared. "It makes me feel ... *uncomfortable*."

"There is certainly a disturbing atmosphere about the thing," Tycho agreed.

"You all sense it, too?" Leandor said. "I thought perhaps it was just me."

"It's obvious, man," Meath told him. "There is power here. Immense power."

"Yes, and a problem to be solved, too," Leandor told him. "It's quite an obvious one actually: I can't read the language the book's written in."

"I've encountered many different tongues in my travels," Meath announced, "and it could be I can help." He reached out for the volume.

"*No!*" Leandor cried, grabbing the mercenary's wrist. "Whatever you do, don't touch it. Any of you. It's dangerous. Kreid was its protector and it killed *him*."

Meath pulled free his hand. "But it won't harm *you*, is that it?"

"It hasn't so far. For the time being at least I'm the only one who's going to handle it."

"But surely that's going to be difficult, given you have only one—"

"Listen!" Shani interrupted. "What's that?"

They heard a deep rumbling. The sound grew rapidly and the floor began to shake.

Tycho pointed to a wall. "Look!"

Irregular cracks were appearing. A cloud of dust fell from the ceiling. Somewhere out of sight, something snapped loudly. On the far side of the room a wide fissure opened in the floor.

"The place is collapsing!" Shani yelled.

Leandor took hold of the book. "We've got to get out of here! *Come on!*"

The chamber lurched crazily as they raced for the exit.

Chapter 21

Slabs of ceiling rained down, walls toppled, cracks zipped across the floor. The noise was deafening, and getting louder.

Tycho took the lead, following the route marked out by the precious thread as chunks of rubble bounced against the glistening floor. Shani came next, hands over her head to protect herself from the bombardment. Leandor, hugging the book to his chest, was close behind. Meath brought up the rear.

They finally got to the end of the maze and began climbing the stairway. It pitched wildly as a succession of tremors tore through the building's fabric. Meath had barely cleared the last step when the staircase collapsed with a thunderous din.

Choking clouds of dust filled the passage leading to the main entrance.

"Hurry!" Shani cried, pointing ahead. "The door!"

The enormous bronze portcullis was descending. It already covered half the opening.

When Tycho reached it, the door was the same height as his head, and coming down faster. He placed his hands against the bottom edge and strained to hold it up. Its progress slowed but didn't stop.

"Be quick!" he shouted. "I cannot do this for long!"

"Use your mind power too!" Shani yelled as she stumbled toward him.

"Yes," the homunculus said. "I will try!" He shut tight his eyes in concentration. The door's downward speed lessened slightly. "But ... I fear ... its weight is ... too great!"

Shani scrambled past him and out into the open.

Leandor arrived, bent double to protect the book. "Hang on, Tycho! Just a few seconds longer!"

Tycho's legs began to buckle. He stooped. The door was at his shoulders now.

"Come on, Meath!" Leandor urged before throwing himself through the exit.

Gasping and coughing, the mercenary staggered into view as Tycho sunk to his knees. The great door creaked ominously. Debris showered them. Meath grunted with the effort of diving to safety.

"Tycho!" Shani screamed.

The homunculus leapt away from his enormous burden. Instantly, the bronze door slammed shut with a resounding crash.

They dashed from the shadow of the crumbling structure. Once clear, they hit the ground and watched as the pyramid rocked, shattered and disintegrated.

With a final violent roar, the green glass structure collapsed in on itself.

Silence returned.

"Thank you, Tycho," Shani said. "We're all grateful for the risk you took."

The others agreed. Then, as he swept dust from his breeches, Meath added, "But, of course, if you are as you say immortal, surely there was no risk of you losing your life, little man?"

"Perhaps not," Tycho replied, "but I did not relish spending the rest of eternity entombed in the ruins."

"Good point," the mercenary conceded. "I wonder what in the world made the pyramid self-destruct?"

"Probably because, like the Guardian, it had the sole purpose of protecting the book," Tycho suggested. "Once that purpose was removed, there was no need for its continued existence."

Shani's eyes fell on the volume, which Leandor still clutched to his chest. "Can we at least look at it, even if we can't touch?"

"Of course." He laid the book on the ground next to him.

"Dalveen!" she exclaimed. "Your wound! It's *gone*!"

Leandor looked down at his chest. Beneath the gash in his shirt the skin was smooth and unbroken. Even the blood had disappeared.

"It can only have been the book," he decided. "I had it against the scar all the way through the maze."

"Then its power is astonishing indeed," Tycho announced. "And if it can heal simply by contact, maybe it would restore your arm in the same way. Why not try it, Dalveen?"

"All right." He stretched out on his side, using the book as though it were a pillow, with the afflicted portion of his body resting on it.

For the better part of an hour they took their ease, exchanging few words, and waited for a sign of the book working its magic.

Finally, Leandor sat up and touched the stump of his missing arm. He couldn't hide his disappointment. "No, nothing," he sighed. "The task obviously requires more than merely being near the thing."

"In that case the answer must lie in the book's knowledge," Meath said. "Let's see if we can make sense of it."

Leandor opened the cover and turned the pages. Before long they had to admit that the text was in a language none of them knew.

He closed it again. "There *has* to be some way of making it do what we want. We'll have to study each page carefully."

"That's all very well," Meath replied, "but this is hardly a suitable place for academic pursuits." He indicated the barren wastes around them with a sweep of his hand. "And you all seem to have forgotten that we're stranded here, with no horses to get us back to the coast. Even if we managed to walk there, how do we then cross the Opal Sea?"

"It could be that the book can help us," Tycho stated.

"This is no time for jokes," the mercenary sneered.

"I'm serious. Avoch-Dar often spoke of how miraculous demon magic was, of how it could do anything if used properly."

"What do you suggest?" Leandor said.

"Well, we could try standing together, touching, while you think of somewhere in Delgarvo you know well."

"This is *ridiculous,*" Meath complained.

Leandor turned to him. "You've felt the power

of the book. You can feel it now. It may seem absurd, but what have we got to lose?"

"Let's try," Shani argued. "If it doesn't work we're no worse off. What place will you concentrate on, Dalveen?"

"Allderhaven's main gate seems as good as any. I must have passed through it hundreds of times. Link hands, everybody. Shani, hold on to my belt on the right side, well away from the book."

They did as he instructed, although Meath took Tycho's furry palm with ill grace.

"I'm thinking of the gate." Leandor had closed his eyes. "I have a clear picture of it in my mind. Hang on, everyone."

A silent half minute passed.

Nothing happened.

"I knew it was stupid," Meath grumbled.

"Why don't you try commanding it, Dalveen?" Shani said.

"I suppose that's as good an idea as any. I wonder what form of words I should use?"

"Just *do* it!" Meath snapped irritably.

"Very well." Leandor cleared his throat. He was starting to feel foolish. "Book! I order you to take us to the main gate of Allderhaven in the land of Delgarvo!"

He had just decided this wasn't going to work either when something strange happened to reality.

The landscape around them began to get hazy, like a view seen through hot air rising on a summer's day. A sound like rushing wind filled his ears. He felt a giddy sensation similar to falling a great distance.

Then a blinding white light seared his eyes and he dropped into a bottomless pit of nothingness.

When Leandor returned to consciousness he was lying on his back.

His head was muzzy and his body ached, but otherwise he seemed uninjured. The book was still clasped to his side. Shani, Tycho and Meath lay close by, and they too were beginning to stir.

He slowly sat up and looked around.

They were in another place.

The desert and the ruined pyramid had gone. Their new surroundings were much lusher, with abundant grass and full-leafed trees. In the middle distance a towering stone wall stretched out of sight to left and right.

"Dalveen?" He turned to see Shani rubbing her eyes. "Where are we?" she asked.

"Delgarvo. Are you all right?"

"I think so. Just a bit wobbly." She scanned the landscape. "It's *incredible.* It worked!"

"Yes. We aren't at Allderhaven's main gate, but it's in walking distance."

Meath and Tycho roused themselves. They took in the scene.

"It seems I was wrong," the mercenary reluctantly admitted. "Perhaps the book *is* capable of anything."

"Yet it hasn't brought us to exactly where we wanted," Tycho noted. "I've never been to Delgarvo before, but this obviously isn't the capital's main gate."

"No," Leandor confirmed, "that lies yonder." He pointed to the wall. "Any idea why that should be so?"

"Perhaps because we simply don't know how to use the book properly yet," the homunculus suggested. "Or it could be that Avoch-Dar is in the city and his magic acted as a kind of barrier that prevented the book getting us any closer."

"Is that possible? I though demon magic was by far the more powerful."

"Do not underestimate the sorcerer's talents. If I know Avoch-Dar, his first act on conquering the city would have been to cast protective spells to keep out unwanted intruders. Had we more knowledge of the book, we probably could have overcome them."

"Still," Meath said, "we're near enough. And apparently none of us has suffered ill effects from being transported here. What do we do now?"

"We get to the city and find a way in," Leandor

told him. "And as it isn't far short of nightfall we start without delay."

They kept away from the main road.

Even so, they expected to encounter people as they passed outlying farms and hamlets. But they saw no one at all.

What they did see was ample evidence of a recent ferocious battle. There were burnt-out buildings, downed fences and trampled crops. Stray cattle roamed the countryside.

"Where *is* everybody?" Tycho wondered.

"In hiding, perhaps," Leandor offered, "or imprisoned. Many could have been killed. Anything's possible after a battle."

"Has anyone noticed how cold it's getting?" Shani asked. "Surely the temperature shouldn't be so low in late spring?"

"You're right," he replied. "Delgarvo's always very mild at this time of year."

The nearer they got to the city, the colder it became. Then a frosty sheen began to appear on the meadows and trees. By the time Allderhaven's walls loomed over them the frost had turned to a layer of ice.

"This isn't natural," Leandor said. "Something's very wrong here."

"I'll wager it has to do with the sorcerer," Tycho declared. "It would come as no surprise to me if the very land about him became as icy as his heart."

They wrapped themselves against the chill as best they could and pushed on.

Night had fallen when they finally reached Allderhaven's main gate.

"It stands ajar, and there don't seem to be any defenders," Leandor observed. "This, too, I have never known."

"We should be wary of tricks," Shani said.

But when they stealthily approached they found no hindrance to entering.

The deserted capital, swathed in ice and bathed by the silvery rays of the moon, had an eerie quality. They kept close to the walls of the streets they walked, alert for any sign of an ambush.

On the barred door of an inn, Tycho came upon a placard and drew their attention to it. "This explains why we haven't seen anybody," he whispered. "It announces a curfew between the hours of dusk and dawn, at penalty of death. It's in the name of Avoch-Dar."

"Then there is no doubt he has taken the city," Leandor said gloomily. "And if there's a curfew there must be patrols to enforce it. So be doubly alert, everyone."

"Dalveen!" Shani hissed from an adjoining door, beckoning him over.

She had found another poster. It read:

A PROCLAMATION

Be it known to all subjects that His Sovereign Lord Avoch-Dar is pleased to announce his betrothal to Princess Bethan of the Imperial House of Eldrick. The wedding ceremony will take place in the Great Hall of the Royal Palace at noon on the second day of the moon's last quarter. All who dwell within the city and its environs are hereby ordered to line the streets for the grand procession following the ceremony. Any person failing to attend or rejoice with sufficient vigour will be put to death.

Leandor gazed at the notice in mute shock.

"It seems affairs have moved on apace," Meath declared.

"I'm so sorry, Dalveen," Shani said softly.

"Unless I'm mistaken," Tycho told them as he looked up at the moon, "the wedding is tomorrow."

CHAPTER 22

"Somebody's coming!"

At Shani's warning, Leandor tore his eyes from the notice. "Where?"

"Other end of the street. Looks like a patrol."

A distant party of soldiers was marching toward them.

He quickly looked around for an escape route and saw the mouth of an alley. "I don't think they've seen us. This way!"

They hurried after him, Meath and Shani with hands close to their blades, Tycho casting a backward glance at the approaching militia.

The alley was ill-lit and shadowy enough to hide in. Flattening themselves against the walls, they prepared for a fight. The sound of boots on cobblestones drew nearer.

But the band of living men and zombie guards passed by, the zombies a little less steady on their shuffling feet than their human comrades.

When he was sure they'd gone, Leandor whispered, "We'll avoid the main thoroughfares from now on." He nodded further along the alley. "This takes us in the direction of Torpoint. Stay alert."

Leandor guided them through the sprawling network of back streets he had known since childhood. After walking silently for ten minutes they came to a fork in the lane. They took the left-hand path, then turned a sharp corner.

And found the way blocked by a group of heavily-armed warriors.

"Damn!" Shani exclaimed, tugging loose a knife.

Meath, almost slipping on the icy cobbles, whipped out his sword.

"Wait!" Leandor ordered.

The figures before them had not moved. They stood in rigid poses, some with weapons drawn, others with hands on the hilts of their blades.

Leandor crept forward. There was just enough murky light for him to identify their uniforms.

"They're the King's men," he said, "members of his personal guard."

The others joined him and examined the ice-coated warriors.

"They are frozen," Tycho confirmed, "but not by the elements. An enchantment holds them in bondage. This is the work of Avoch-Dar."

Leandor was staring at one of the fighters, a massively-built, full-bearded officer of mature years.

"*Oh no,*" he whispered.

"What is it, Dalveen?" Shani asked.

"It's Golcar. Golcar Quixwood, my adoptive father."

Meath studied the blue-tinged faces. "Are they dead?"

Shani, realizing Leandor had no free hand unless he put down the book, reached out and touched a vein in Quixwood's neck. "No. There's a pulse. It's faint, but regular."

Tycho clasped the wrist of another man. "Same here. No doubt my ex-master intends killing them at his leisure. It would appeal to his twisted sense of humour to keep them in this undignified state until then."

"Perhaps the book could help," Shani suggested.

"That's exactly what I was thinking," Leandor replied. "Book, I order you to release these men."

The warriors did not move.

"You didn't really expect such a basic command to work, did you?" Meath sneered.

"It was worth trying. Do you have a better idea?"

"Or it could be Avoch-Dar's countering magic

again," Tycho said. "If so, the closer we get to the sorcerer the more powerful it's likely to become."

"We should push on," Meath stated.

"I can't just leave Golcar!" Leandor flared.

"What do you suggest, *carrying* him? Such a burden would guarantee our capture, man."

"Meath's right, Dalveen," Shani said gently. "The best thing we can do for Golcar and these others is to attack the source of the spell that binds them. Come on, we've done all we can here."

"All right," he sighed.

He took a last look at Quixwood's impassive face before reluctantly leading them into the night.

Tycho wrapped the chain around his powerful paws and snapped it.

Shani cautiously pushed open the door and looked in. "It seems empty," she whispered. "But Meath and I should check first. Stay here until we get back."

A minute later she returned to usher Leandor and Tycho into the humble dwelling.

"From the state of the place it was abandoned in a hurry," Meath reported. He secured the door by propping a piece of wood against it. "There's just two rooms, and the one at the rear has a window, should we need to make a quick exit."

"Perfect," Leandor said.

He placed the book on a large table, one of the

room's few pieces of furniture, while Tycho collected the scattered chairs.

Shani dipped a hand into a wooden barrel in the corner and licked her fingers. "There's water. It's a bit brackish but drinkable."

"And this bread isn't more than a couple of days old," Meath announced, taking a black, brick-shaped loaf from a nearby shelf.

They sat for their frugal meal and discussed what to do next.

"The first thing I want to say," Leandor told them, "is that now we're back in Delgarvo, none of you are obliged to stay with me. You've risked your lives enough times already. I'll quite understand if you want no more to do with my fight against Avoch-Dar."

"It isn't just your fight," Shani said. "We all have reasons for wanting to see the wizard overthrown." She exchanged glances with Tycho and Meath. "We're with you all the way."

"Thank you." He smiled. "But make no mistake, things are going to get even rougher from this point, and our chances of success are pretty slim."

"We know that," Tycho replied.

"I would have liked more time to come up with some kind of plan," Leandor continued. "But finding out about the wedding, and knowing Golcar is trapped out there, has forced my hand."

"So what *do* you intend doing?" Meath asked.

"I'm not sure. Try to rescue Bethan, I suppose."

Tycho's gaze went to the Book of Shadows. "It seems to me that everything Melva told you has proved right so far," he said thoughtfully. "What did she have to say about how to use the book?"

"As I recall, the same thing she said about finding it; that the answer would be obvious."

"Trust her word. Let the book guide you."

"How?"

"Well, instead of *consciously* looking for the correct way, try letting your instinct take over. You might start by opening the volume at random."

"It's worth a try. Help me clear the table."

They swept aside everything but the book.

"Empty your mind," Tycho suggested, "and begin when you feel ready."

Leandor stood in quiet contemplation for a moment. Then he reached out and opened the tome without thought. The pages revealed had very little on them. On the left was a simple illustration; on the right a single sentence of just six words.

"The drawing's of a bird of some sort," Shani commented, "but it only has one wing. *Oh.*" She fell silent on realizing its significance.

"It's a hawk," Leandor whispered.

"Does this mean anything to you?" Tycho asked. "Apart from the obvious symbolism of the missing wing, that is?"

"The mountain where I took refuge before

embarking on the quest was called Hawkstone. And … it was where Melva lived."

"This is beyond a coincidence," the homunculus stated. "And note that the writing on the facing page is much nearer our own language than anything else we've seen in the book. The words mean nothing to me, but you should have no difficulty reading them aloud."

"Have a care, Leandor," Meath warned. "This is *demon* magic you're dealing with. You don't know what you might be unleashing!"

"I've not come this far to give up now. But it could be wise for you all to stand back at this point."

They moved to the other side of the room.

He took a deep breath and laid his hand on the page bearing the likeness of a hawk.

Then he recited the words.

"Ex Umbris et Imaginibus in Veritatem!"

And screamed.

Avoch-Dar gasped.

It was like someone had plunged a blistering needle into his heart. He clutched his chest and staggered into the banqueting table. Fine china and crystalware smashed against the floor.

The Captain of his Guard rushed forward to aid him. He swiped the man away and cursed viciously. Clutching the table to support himself, the wizard struggled to catch his breath.

Princess Bethan looked on in horrified fascination. Her ladies in waiting, the drawn-out train of her black wedding gown in their hands, were pallid with shock.

"He has ... found ... the way..." he panted.

"He?" Bethan said.

"Nightshade! Your ... precious Leandor! He ... has found the ... way to use ... the book! I ... feel it! Its power is ... awesome!"

The Princess smiled. "I do not know the book you speak of. But I do know that Dalveen will avenge the wrongs you have done me, fiend!"

"Silence!"

From the look he wore she knew it best to still her tongue.

The sorcerer was regaining control. "It ... is no more ... than I expected." He gradually straightened and began to breathe normally. "I can see from ... your expression that ... you are concerned with my ... well-being, my lady," he added sarcastically. "But have no fear. I ... am unharmed."

She scowled at him.

"The power of the book is indeed stunning," he went on, "as I knew it would be. And it must be near! You!" The command was directed at the trembling Captain. "Organize a search," the sorcerer ordered, "and put every available man into it. Bring Nightshade to me."

The officer bowed and ran for the door.

"And if you fail," Avoch-Dar shouted at his back, "you will wish you had never been born!"

* * *

"What's *happening* to him?" Shani said, panic rising in her voice.

Leandor's upper body was slumped over the table. The first, ear-splitting scream had given way to racking, throaty moans. He writhed uncontrollably, his legs kicking.

And a pulse of ghostly blue light shimmered around the stump of his missing arm.

"We've got to help!" She tried to reach him, but Tycho held her in an iron grip.

"Be sensible, girl!" Meath snapped. "He's subject to demonic magic. If you go near you risk death. Or worse!"

"We can only wait and watch," Tycho told her, "much as it pains us to do so."

Leandor groaned loudly. The throbbing blue radiance grew stronger and more rapid. Between the bursts of rhythmic light the ghostly outline of a limb appeared where none had been before.

The light became so powerful they had to cover their faces.

Then a blast of dazzling brilliance exploded with the intensity of a lightning bolt.

It was immediately followed by the return of the previous gloom.

They lowered their hands. Despite shielding their eyes they felt as if they had been staring into the sun.

Shani blinked to clear the glare. Leandor was lying prone across the table. "My gods," she gasped, "he's dead!"

But as they slowly approached he stirred. And they saw that his arm had not been renewed.

"Are you all right?" Tycho asked.

Leandor lifted his gaze from the stump and regarded them with feverish eyes. Sweat soaked his face. He laboured for air.

Shani laid her hand gently on his back. "Dalveen?" she said.

The glazed look went from his eyes and he focused on her. "Is it ... true?" he whispered. "Have I failed?"

"I'm afraid so, Dalveen. The book has not restored your arm. I'm ... sorry."

Leandor gave her a look of utter despair.

Tycho and Meath managed to catch him before he fell unconscious to the floor.

Chapter 23

By dawn, Leandor had recovered physically. But his mood was bleak.

"At least you came close," Shani reassured him. "We all saw it. For a few seconds the outline of your missing limb was visible. Take comfort from that."

"I'm sure the only reason your arm wasn't restored is because we don't yet know how to use the book properly, Dalveen," Tycho added.

"Perhaps you're right," Leandor sighed. "It's just ... well, I had such high hopes that it would make me complete again." He drew his sword from its sheath on the table and with lightning speed carved a figure eight in the air. "I was always a natural right-hander when it came to swordplay. Using my left is something I've never been entirely happy with."

"Necessity has served you well," Meath observed. "You're as good as any man I've seen, despite your loss."

"But am I good *enough*? That's the question." The look of brooding intensity returned to his face.

"We all sympathize with you, Dalveen," Tycho told him. "But the wedding is in less than six hours and we have yet to come up with a plan."

Leandor returned the sword to its scabbard. "Of course. Forgive me."

"It's understandable," Shani said. "But Tycho's right. What's our first move?"

"We should see if the book can get us past Avoch-Dar's magic and into the palace."

"I wouldn't be too hopeful," Tycho stated as they linked hands.

He was right. Nothing happened when Leandor gave the command for them to be transported inside the castle's walls. He put the book down and said, "We'll have to find another way."

"Is there one?" Meath asked.

"I was brought up in Torpoint, remember, and I know of a way in. Assuming it hasn't been discovered and blocked, that is. Shall we make ready to leave?"

"Hold your horses," Shani cautioned. "There are one or two things we've got to do first."

"Such as?"

"Well, there's Tycho for a start." She turned to him. "No offence, but your appearance is hardly ... *normal*. If you go on the streets looking like that we'll be picked up in minutes."

"It is a good point," the homunculus agreed. "But how do you suggest I disguise myself?"

"I found this." She took a needle and a ball of thread from her pocket. "I could put something together from the bedding in the other room."

"You want me to go out wearing *blankets*?"

"It wouldn't take long to turn one into a sort of robe, and make a hood out of another. You could pass for a holy man. You'd have to keep your hands out of sight though."

Leandor approved. "Excellent idea, Shani. What else?"

"The book. Wouldn't it be best to hide it somewhere?"

"That would be unwise!" Meath blurted.

"It certainly would," Leandor agreed. "No matter how well we hid it, there's a risk of it being found, and it's too dangerous for that. No, it stays with me."

"All right," Shani said. "We'll find a piece of material to wrap it in. And we're going to need a makeshift cloak to hide your missing arm, Dalveen."

"Yes," he murmured darkly, "it rather gives me

away, doesn't it?"

Shani almost commented on the bitterness in his voice, but thought better of it. Instead she reached for the darning materials and said, "Let's get started, shall we?"

The people trudging Allderhaven's ice-bound streets looked afraid and dejected. And the unnatural cold added to their misery.

"Not much joy for a wedding day, is there?" Shani said.

Leandor tightened his hold on the sack-covered book. "You can almost *taste* the fear." He glanced at his sword, now at his waist because of the makeshift cloak he wore. "Be on the lookout for patrols, everyone."

"I am having enough difficulty trying to see where I'm going," Tycho complained from the depths of his baggy costume. His face was barely visible inside the cowl.

"At least you should be warm in there," Shani teased.

"Extremes of temperature do not bother me," he replied huffily.

They came to a ragged line of roadside stalls selling bread and fruit.

"Fresh food," Meath enthused. "Hold a moment while I buy some."

"At a time like *this*?" Shani grumbled.

"I can't remember when we last had anything decent to eat. And where possible I make it a rule to feed the inner man before a battle." He swaggered off, digging into his pockets for a coin.

The others kept walking in order not to attract attention. They stopped to wait for him in a doorway opposite the last stall. When Leandor glanced back, Meath was haggling with one of the vendors.

An elderly man walked past, staring hard at Leandor's sword. Shani caught his eye and he quickly dropped his gaze.

She snapped her fingers. "Damn! I wondered why people were looking at us."

"What's wrong?"

"It's your sword. No one we've seen is wearing a weapon. They've obviously been outlawed. Hide it!"

He swept forward his cloak to cover the scabbard. "That was a stupid mistake. Fortunately you and Tycho are all right."

"But Meath isn't!" the homunculus exclaimed. "His blade is in plain view!"

"I'll tell him," Shani offered.

"No!" Leandor cautioned. "Look!"

A group of soldiers had come around the corner next to Meath's stall. The officer leading them noticed him. He barked an order. His men drew their weapons and rushed to surround the mercenary.

"Hell's teeth!" Shani hissed.

The officer and Meath were arguing. The argument became a struggle. He was seized and disarmed.

Shani fingered her sleeve. "Do we pitch in?"

"There's at least a dozen," Leandor said, "and who knows how many more nearby. If we're all captured the game's up. Dammit, we *can't* help him!"

They withdrew further into the doorway as Meath was bundled off at swordpoint.

"What do you think they'll do with him?" Shani asked.

"They're taking him toward the palace. When they get there, who knows? But there's no reason to link him with us."

"Don't be too sure," Tycho offered. "They could break him with torture. Avoch-Dar has some ingenious ways of making people talk."

"Now *there's* a pleasant thought," Shani said grimly.

Torpoint looked like a palace of ice. Its towers stood white and stark against the brooding sky.

They had seen more groups of frozen warriors on the way. And the nearer they came to the palace, the greater their numbers. Fearful of the roaming patrols, Allderhaven's citizens shunned these bands of motionless fighters, and even avoided looking at them.

Leandor, Shani and Tycho had to change direction several times to evade guards, but eventually arrived at the castle walls. In a quiet side street, Leandor showed them a small iron gate.

"This leads to the royal gardens," he explained. "Can you get us in, Tycho?"

"I think so. Keep watch while I try." He pressed his brawny shoulder against the gate and pushed. The lock snapped and it swung open.

When Leandor was sure there was no one about they dashed across the frosty lawn to another wall. He guided them into a thicket of bushes.

"What we're looking for is around here somewhere... Ah, there!" He tapped his foot on a square metal cover set in the ground. "We need your strength again, Tycho."

The hatch lifted easily. Beneath was a shallow tunnel.

"What is it?" Shani asked.

"An old rain duct, part of a system that carries water away from the ramparts above. This is a short section leading to the interior courtyard."

She stared down into the darkness. A trickling sound could be heard. "I'm not keen on tunnels. Let's get it over with."

"Before we do, remember, the plan is to locate Bethan and the King and free them. If we can find Meath too, that's a bonus."

"It's a tall order," Tycho said. "If we succeed, have you given any thought to what happens then?"

"We get out of the city and use the King as a rallying point for an uprising against the sorcerer. It isn't the best plan in the world, but it's all I can think of."

They nodded.

"This tunnel is only big enough for us to go single-file," he continued. "As there's another hatch to be opened at the other end, it'd be best for you to go first, Tycho."

The artificial man awkwardly lowered himself through the opening. "It's very icy down here," he called. "Be careful."

Leandor lowered the sack containing the book and descended. Shani followed, lugging the cover back into place behind her with a grunt of effort.

They splashed along, bent double, in the pitch black. Before long they reached a wall.

"The hatch's directly above," Leandor pointed out. "Just lift it a little and see if anybody's around."

Tycho applied upward pressure, letting in a crack of light. "It seems clear." He pushed away the cover as quietly as he could and climbed out. Then he hoisted them after him. As they scanned the courtyard for signs of life, he replaced it.

"This way," Leandor whispered. He headed

across the flagstones to a door in the side of the palace.

It was unlocked. They drew their weapons and slipped in, craning their heads left and right. The spacious corridors were deserted.

"Where do we go?" Tycho said.

"The Great Hall seems a good place to start. Along here."

"I'm glad you know the way," Shani whispered. "This place is a warren."

They came to a grand passage ending in a pair of enormous doors. Leandor crept to them. "I don't know what we're going to find in here, but if it's anything we can't cope with, *run*." He turned the brass handle and shoved.

The huge room was empty. Its dining table, running nearly the entire length of one end of the chamber, was laid out for the wedding banquet. They entered and looked around.

"What now?" Shani wondered.

"Now you are mine!"

They spun to face the door.

Avoch-Dar stood in the entrance.

Scores of his men, heavily armed, poured in behind him and spread out around the room.

"How very obliging of you to walk into my hands, Nightshade," he gloated. "Now put down your weapons."

"Like *hell*!" Shani spat. "I knew we got into this

place too easily!" She drew a second knife. One in each hand, she made ready to fight.

"Don't expect a meek surrender, Avoch-Dar," Leandor promised. "If we're to die, we're taking as many as possible with us!"

The wizard laughed. "I don't think so. Bring them in!"

Princess Bethan was marched into the room by two guards. One held a dagger to her throat. *"Dalveen!"* she gasped, trying to hide the terror in her face.

"Bethan!"

Next came the King, prodded in at swordpoint.

"I repeat," Avoch-Dar said. "Lay down your weapons."

"Don't surrender, Dalveen!" the King shouted. "Our lives are of no consequence! Sell yours dearly!"

"Silence, you old cretin!" Avoch-Dar demanded. "Unless you want to see the colour of your daughter's blood!"

Leandor sighed. He looked to his companions, then tossed his sword to the floor. Shani dropped her knives.

The sorcerer greedily eyed the bundle Leandor clutched. "I take it that is ... the book. Place it on the table. Put it down, I say!"

Bethan gave a sharp intake of breath as the guard pressed his dagger deeper into her flesh.

Leandor laid the book on the table, sweeping crockery aside. He peeled away the sacking.

Avoch-Dar strode over. "Open it!" he commanded.

Leandor lifted the cover and began turning the pages.

"Fascinating," the sorcerer whispered.

"You can read this?"

"I have spent years studying surviving fragments of the demons' language. Keep turning the pages."

They were near the end before Avoch-Dar found what he wanted. "Excellent! The spell supreme. Now back off!"

When Leandor did as he was told, the guards moved in and seized him and his companions. Shani's arm scabbards were roughly torn away. The homunculus's makeshift garments were ripped from his body.

"Ah yes, my loyal servant Tycho. Welcome back," the wizard mocked. He nodded to an officer by the door. The man leaned out and beckoned someone. "And now I think a reunion is in order."

Craigo Meath appeared.

"Meath!" Shani exclaimed. "Are you all right? Have they harmed you?"

The mercenary smiled. Unpleasantly.

"Allow me to introduce my lieutenant," Avoch-Dar announced.

Shani gaped at them. "Your *what*?"

"You see before you, young lady, one of my most trusted servants."

"What have they done to you, Meath? Say it isn't true!"

"Still your tongue, *girl*!" the mercenary sneered.

"What did it take, Meath?" Leandor said coldly. "The promise of riches? Power? What was your price for turning against us?"

"You fool, Leandor. I have served but one master from the start."

"A traitor all along, is that it? I *was* a fool not to have seen it."

"But you fought with us," Shani argued. "You saved Dalveen's life!"

"Only because it was his job to do so," Avoch-Dar replied. "Meath's task was to do all he could to ensure the book came to *me*. Even at the cost of preserving Nightshade's life."

"And how I hated that part of it!" There was acid in Meath's voice. "You have no idea what joy it would have given me to let that sea creature tear you apart, Leandor, or to have watched you drown. How hard I fought with myself not to plunge my blade into your back at every opportunity."

"You rat!" Shani screamed, struggling against the arms that restrained her. "Stabbing a man in the back is just about your level, isn't it?"

"Why didn't you just point us out in the street

and have done with it, Meath?" Tycho asked.

"It was a genuine arrest. The patrol captain didn't know who I was until he got me here. The idiot! And if I had denounced you, there would probably have been a fight. I couldn't run the risk of you escaping with the book."

"It also gave you another reason to come here, Nightshade," Avoch-Dar added. "The noble hero chancing all to rescue his betrothed and his supposed friend. You can be terribly predictable, you know."

Leandor fixed the wizard with a frigid gaze. "So you used us to obtain the book. Of course, you had to. Melva the wise woman said that only the pure of heart could gain it. That certainly left *you* out, didn't it?"

"It did present a problem. But you have solved that, as I intended. Now I will employ the demon race's secrets to increase my magical powers beyond all imagining! Regrettably, you and your friends will not be here to see it."

"No doubt your cowardly lieutenant will take care of that," Shani told him. "With a knife in our backs!"

"Oh, I had something much more inventive in mind. But you have given me an idea that may provide some amusement. Meath, how would you like to cross blades with the legendary Nightshade?"

"It would give me the greatest pleasure, master." He shot Leandor a vicious look. "My skill is more than equal to this so-called champion!"

"Give me your rapier," the sorcerer ordered.

The traitor passed it over. Avoch-Dar held it in one hand. The other, palm flat, he ran along the length of the blade as he muttered a dark incantation. A sparkly blue glow surrounded the sword for a second, then faded away.

"To make things more interesting," the wizard explained, "I have cast an enchantment upon this blade so that its merest *touch* means certain death to all but its user." He handed it back to Meath. Then he turned to Leandor and said, "Now take up your weapon, Nightshade."

"And if I don't?"

"You'll watch your friends suffer a lingering death."

Dalveen hesitated for a second, then retrieved his sword from the floor.

The crowd fell back.

Meath stepped forward, a twisted smile on his lips. "I'm going to enjoy this," he smirked.

He raised the lethal blade and moved in to attack.

Chapter 24

Captors and captives looked on in silence as the two men warily circled each other.

Then Meath lunged forward and their swords met with a resounding crash.

The sound of ringing steel echoed through the Great Hall as they exchanged blow for blow. They fought grimly, neither taking a step in retreat, each seeking an opening in the other's defences.

Meath slashed at Leandór, the deadly blade so close to his head its passing ruffled his hair. He came back with an upward swipe that, unleashed a heartbeat sooner, would have severed the mercenary's arm.

Their singing blades cleaved the air and clashed

again. Leandor danced to one side, ducked and directed a thrust at Meath's thigh. His opponent dodged, spun and struck out at Leandor's face. Quick reflexes and sheer luck avoided a hit.

They fenced to and fro across the white marble floor, the crowd parting to make way for them. Every move Leandor made, Meath parried, and the mercenary's attacks were likewise fended off. They hacked and slashed without let, heedless of all others, their duel ranging to one end of the room and back.

And Leandor was ever aware that the lightest touch of his opponent's blade meant certain death.

Meath launched a fresh onslaught with renewed frenzy. Leandor moved in to counter it. They traded stroke for stroke in a dazzling exhibition of swordplay that brought gasps from friend and foe alike.

The duel was so frantic that both men were already tiring and couldn't keep up the pace much longer.

As he kicked a chair from his path, Leandor caught a glimpse of Avoch-Dar. From his expression the sorcerer was hugely amused by the spectacle. Then Meath swung a body-cut and it was back to the fray.

Limbs aching, lungs seared with effort, Dalveen plumbed the depths of his being for the strength to battle on.

Their fight took them to within a few paces of where the King and Bethan were held. The guards, engrossed by the martial display, had let attention wander from their charges. Out of the corner of his eye, Leandor saw a flurry of movement.

The King had broken away. His surprised escorts were slow to react and pursue him. With the agility of someone years younger, Eldrick leapt up and snatched an ornamental spear attached to the wall.

He thrust the lance at the first guard. It penetrated the man's chain-mail and he spiralled to the floor. The second approached slowly with raised sword.

Eldrick ignored him, drew back the spear and hurled it at Meath. But the mercenary swerved in time to avoid the soaring weapon. It clattered uselessly on the far side of the room.

The second guard rushed in and delivered a vicious slash to the old man's chest.

"Father!" Bethan screamed.

Eldrick slumped to his knees.

When Meath spun around to continue the fight he wore a wicked grin of triumph and contempt.

Ungovernable fury rose in Leandor's breast. His vision flooded with a scarlet haze. The insanity of berserk rage gripped him.

With eye-blurring speed he swerved away from Meath and turned on the terrified guard. One stroke dashed the sword from his hand. The next caved in his ribs. He was dead before he hit the floor.

It happened so fast Meath couldn't react. Then Leandor was back to him, smashing into the mercenary's defences. All pretence at civilized combat had vanished now. Leandor surrendered entirely to Nightshade, the avenger of wrongs, the ultimate Champion.

The savage killer.

Meath faced a tempest of murderous flashing steel. His arrogant smirk gave way to apprehension. Then dismay. Then naked terror.

He retreated, struggling to fend off the storm of stinging blows that rained down on him. His back struck the edge of the grand dining table. The rapier was knocked aside, leaving him defenceless.

Meath saw nothing but pitiless wrath in his conqueror's eyes.

"Mercy!" he begged.

"There *is* no mercy for the agents of evil," Leandor told him.

And drove his blade deep into the traitor's heart.

Leandor stepped back and watched as Meath sank to the floor, rolled once and came to rest. A pool of blood spread from the lifeless body.

The hush was broken by the sound of a pair of hands slow clapping.

Leandor blinked away the crimson glare of

anger and looked around. Avoch-Dar was the source of the false tribute.

"An excellent entertainment," the sorcerer said.

"Do you not regret the loss of your lieutenant?" Leandor panted.

"Not especially. He has served his purpose. As have you. So give up your weapon."

The wizard's men edged toward Leandor. He hesitated, pondering whether to make a stand and end it here.

Avoch-Dar pointed to Shani and the others. "If you resist, it goes the harder on them."

Once more, Leandor threw down his sword.

"And now to more pressing business," the wizard announced, striding to the table.

He gazed at the open book.

Leandor began walking in the direction of the fallen King. The guards pressed in and levelled their weapons at him.

The wizard glanced over. "Let them have a last few minutes together," he ordered absently. "They can do us no harm." He returned his attention to the book.

Released, Bethan ran to Leandor's arms. Together, they went to her father and found him alive. Tycho and Shani joined them. A semicircle of guards kept suspicious watch over the anxious group.

The Princess knelt beside the King and took his

hand. A tear made its way down her cheek. "Father," she sobbed, "oh, father..."

The monarch smiled weakly. *"Don't ... weep for ... me, daughter. I'm ... tougher ... than ... you think."* He paused to fight for breath, then turned his noble head to Leandor. *"You ... have done ... well, Dalveen. Do not ... do ... not ... give up ... yet!"* He drifted into semi-consciousness.

"He's right," Shani said. "We should not go meekly to our deaths."

"We have no weapons," Leandor reminded her.

"Then we'll fight with our bare hands." She glanced at the sentries. "If I'm going to hell I'm taking a few of these devils with me!"

Bethan dabbed her eyes. "Your friend has spirit, Dalveen."

The two young women regarded each other, both proud in their own way.

The moment ended when Avoch-Dar addressed the room.

"I have decided to make use of the book immediately," he announced, "and to bring forth its creators from the dimension in which they now dwell!"

An excited buzz of whispers swept the crowd.

"Our ... *guests* – " he nodded toward Leandor and the other captives – "will be offered to them as sacrifices. From what I know of the demon race, that will be appreciated."

A ripple of laughter ran through the ranks of the wizard's followers.

"The demons were the most powerful magical race this world has ever seen," he went on. "I will compel them to bestow some of that power on me. But before I begin, a precaution is necessary."

Avoch-Dar went to Meath's body. He dipped a cloth in the widening pool of blood, then began to draw a shape on the floor with it. At his command, two guards came forward to soak further cloths and pass them to him as needed.

In ten minutes the sorcerer had painted a large red pentagram on the white marble.

"Were anyone to step into this circle," he explained, "its magic would be broken. It could no longer prevent the demons entering our world and wreaking havoc. Perhaps they would not obey even *my* orders. So I have fashioned it in such a way that no human *can* cross the line."

All were silent as he returned to the book. Bethan squeezed Leandor's hand. Shani clutched his arm. Tension was heavy in the chamber.

Avoch-Dar stared at the open tome for a few seconds before he started to read the words aloud. The language was strange and unintelligible to those listening. But they needed no translation to understand that the rite he performed was black and terrible.

As he came to the end of the incantation, a dark,

swirling haze began to form in the centre of the pentagram. The acrid smell of sulphur drifted across the chamber. An eerie red and gold glow pulsated in the dense murk.

In the core of the cloud a mass of shapes took on solidity.

CHAPTER 25

Leandor had expected all the demons to look alike.

As the mist cleared he realized he was wrong.

And he saw that they were more horrible than the denizens of any nightmare.

No two creatures within the crowded circle seemed to have the same appearance. The impression was of leathery wings, writhing tentacles, curled horns, prickly tails and cloven hooves. Some had scales, some were hairless and warty, some were covered in spiky fur.

Among the seething host were beings resembling huge bats, toads and beetles. He saw one that was part serpent and part lion, another half bear and half bird of prey.

Five-legged dwarves jostled spindly giants sporting multiple pairs of arms. There were demons with leering skulls, the heads of horses, snakes and rats. Many had more than one head, including a beast with the body of a crocodile topped by three snarling dogs.

Others were so terrible they defied description.

Bethan's fingers dug into Leandor's flesh. Shani gasped in shock.

King Eldrick, ashen-faced, whispered, *"If ... Avoch-Dar ... succeeds in gaining ... the power he seeks, all ... human life ... is ... in peril!"*

The demon horde radiated a menace that was almost tangible. Even the sorcerer's followers looked upon them with undisguised fear.

"Are they not wondrous to behold?" Avoch-Dar proclaimed, his voice filled with awe. He approached the circle and commanded, "As possessor of the book, I order you to do my bidding! I demand ultimate magical power!"

Scores of dreadful eyes coldly regarded him.

"All's lost!" Bethan exclaimed.

"Perhaps not, my lady," Tycho told her. "There is one slim chance."

"What do you mean?" Leandor asked.

"Wish me luck!" the homunculus said, quickly scrambling to his feet.

He began running.

The guards were so taken with the unfolding

drama that Tycho was through them before they reacted. By the time they did, they found he wasn't easy to stop. Blows from swords bounced harmlessly off his toughened hide and spear thrusts were deflected. An arrow directed at his back snapped in two.

Shani was baffled. "What does he hope to achieve?"

"I think I know," Leandor replied. "And if he manages it, be ready for mayhem!"

Tycho dashed past Avoch-Dar and across the pentagram's outer edge.

Then immediately turned and ran out again.

The protective spell of the circle was shattered.

Demons instantly poured through the breach. And as they spilled into the Great Hall others appeared in the glowing portal at the pentagram's heart and followed them.

Hell was let loose in Torpoint.

Avoch-Dar roared with rage as the hideous creatures tore into his militia. Shouts, screams and utterly inhuman sounds filled the room. Bloody chaos reigned.

"Come on!" Leandor yelled.

He leapt at a nearby guard, felled him and wrestled away his sword.

"A blade!" Shani cried. "Give me a *blade*!"

Leandor cut down a fleeing sentry, snatched his rapier and tossed it to her. She caught it by the hilt and ran it through an approaching guardsman.

Already the floor was littered with the bodies of the dead and dying. The demons were unstoppable, ripping at human flesh, batting away swords and lances. And when they were hit, the blows had no noticeable effect.

"Stand watch over Bethan and the King!" Leandor cried. He raced toward the sorcerer.

As she turned to obey, Shani was in near collision with an archer and brought him down with a swipe of her sword. Preferring his weapon, she snatched the man's bow and quiver. Avoch-Dar was still in plain view so she notched an arrow and sent it winging his way. It missed narrowly, embedding itself in a wall tapestry.

She returned to Eldrick and the Princess, and found Tycho there, shielding them from the tumult.

Hacking through the confused mass, Leandor came within sight of the magician. Avoch-Dar brought up his hands and unleashed a dazzling bolt of energy. Leandor jumped to one side. The sizzling fireball exploded against a wall.

He pushed on again as the sorcerer flung another burning bolt. Wide of its mark, it struck several of his own men. Shrieking, they were enveloped in flames.

Leandor was distracted by the sight, and the

necessity of dealing with a guard unwise enough to engage him in swordplay. By the time he looked to the wizard once more he saw him surrounded by a pack of demons. He seemed to be talking to them, or perhaps reciting a ritual, but Leandor could not hear his words.

Then Avoch-Dar and the demons began moving to the pentagram.

Leandor tracked them from a safe distance, fighting off the few soldiers who tried to stop him. There were fewer people blocking his path now, and more corpses to be stepped over, most of the guards having perished or fled.

The nightmare band with Avoch-Dar at its core reached the pentagram.

Other demons were making their way back to the magic circle, and Leandor was careful to stay clear of them. But he noticed that one particularly repulsive creature stood at the banqueting table, looking down at the Book of Shadows. Slamming shut the volume, it scooped it up in its scaly claws.

For the briefest of seconds, the demon's appalling eyes met Leandor's. He saw all the terrors of the pit there, all the torment endured by damned souls, and shuddered.

Then the demon clutched the book to its slimy chest and slithered off to join the rest of the host.

Dalveen was filled with despair. He could see

his only hope of salvation being taken from him. After all he and his comrades had been through, all the suffering, hardship and death, he was being forced to watch as the book was snatched away. And his gloating enemy was about to escape. For Leandor knew his feeble human strength was no match for the brutal might of the hellish creatures.

Yet still he rushed forward.

He got to the magical ring just after the demon with the book entered it. In a frenzy of desperation he threw aside his sword and thrust his hand across the line of blood, hoping to seize the tome.

It was as though he had plunged his fist into molten lava.

The pain was too great. He stifled a scream and pulled back his blistering arm.

An insane, triumphant laugh rang out. Avoch-Dar, amid the ghastly throng, mocked Leandor's agony and hopelessness.

The air in the infernal circle thickened and grew misty. The shimmering red and gold haze returned.

Then there was a silent explosion of intense, blinding light. A heatwave struck Leandor, knocking him to the ground.

And the pentagram was empty.

"Will you stop *fussing,* man!" the King complained.

"You really should try to be more co-operative with your physician, father," Bethan told him. She nodded at the doctor. He bowed and backed out of the bedchamber.

"Thank the gods your injury wasn't more serious," she added. "In another week or two you'll be on your feet again."

"If you think I'm staying cooped up in bed that long, you're mistaken! It takes more than a scratch to lay me low."

"Your injury is hardly a *scratch,* sire," Golcar Quixwood said. "Try being a good patient."

"That won't come easy, old friend. But tell me, how are you feeling yourself?"

"Fine. As soon as the sorcerer vanished, the enchantment that kept me and the Imperial Guard in suspended animation was broken. There don't seem to be any after-effects."

"I'm pleased to hear it. How goes the mopping-up operation?"

"We're near to rooting out the last of Avoch-Dar's forces. Without their leader they're too dispirited to put up much of a fight. As to the lifeless ones, his zombie warriors, they returned to death when he went. Again, the spell that held them was broken."

"You know," the King said, "I can't help thinking of earlier times, the days when Avoch-Dar was a trusted servant. If he hadn't been so weak he would never have allowed himself to be corrupted by the dark side of magic."

"If I may say so, Your Majesty," Tycho stated, "your sympathy is misplaced. I believe the wizard carried a seed of evil from the start, that he was born to wreak havoc. It would fit with what we know of the prophecy."

"Perhaps you're right," Eldrick allowed. "In any event, we have much to thank you for. Your quick thinking saved the day."

"There's no doubt of that," Bethan agreed. "You were clear-headed enough to realize that Avoch-Dar's spell didn't apply to you."

"Thank you, my lady. Yes, he overlooked me, as he always did. As I am not human, there was nothing to stop me breaching the pentagram."

"But surely, Tycho, in breaking the circle didn't you imperil human life?" Shani asked. "I thought you weren't able to do that."

"No, I simply crossed a line of blood on the floor. I did not directly put any human's life in danger. Certainly not Avoch-Dar's, for his dabbling in the darker realms of magic had made him less than human anyway."

"You will be rewarded for your valour," the King promised. "And from now on you are under royal protection. There will be some kind of role for you here in the palace, if you want it."

"I am honoured, sire."

Eldrick's expression grew sombre. "And what of Dalveen? How does he fare?"

"As you would expect," Bethan replied sadly, "he's greatly depressed at the turn of events. To have his hopes dashed that way, and to see the foul wizard elude justice, were cruel blows. I think he –"

She stopped at the sound of the opening door.

Leandor entered, his only arm and hand heavily bandaged. It was plain how downcast he felt.

"Ah, Dalveen," greeted the King. "We were just speaking of you. How is your wound?"

"It will heal."

"You must try not to brood, my dear," Bethan said.

"Good advice," their monarch agreed. "Avoch-Dar may not have been defeated, but you and your friends *did* foil his scheme to conquer Delgarvo. And he was driven to take refuge in whatever infernal realm the demons inhabit."

Leandor turned his vexed eyes to the King. "Yes. But for how long? And wherever he is, he has the book. He's deprived me of the only chance I had to be whole again."

"Not necessarily," Eldrick said. "There are many healers in my kingdom, and we'll consult them all if need be. We're far from giving up yet."

"Thank you, Your Majesty." There was no mistaking his lack of conviction.

"Be of good heart," Quixwood put in. "There is always hope, and we will find a way."

A thin smile came to Leandor's lips. "Perhaps we will."

"Let's look on the bright side," the King continued. "The immediate peril has been overcome, even if only for the present. We must see to it that our defences are as strong as possible should the sorcerer ever threaten us again. There is much to do, Dalveen, and we need you now as much as we ever did."

Leandor's mood lightened a little more at these words. "As you say, sire, there is work to be done."

"It would be best for father to get some rest," Bethan announced. "Golcar and I shall stay with him for a while."

Outside, Tycho made a discreet excuse, leaving Shani and Leandor alone.

She laid her hand gently on his bound arm. "There was wisdom in the King's words, Dalveen. It could be best if you busied yourself helping him rebuild after the destruction Avoch-Dar brought about."

"I will. I'm convinced we haven't seen the last of the sorcerer and we need to be ready." He frowned. "But there's ... something else. Something that puzzles me."

"What's that?"

"Come, I'll show you."

He lead her along the corridor toward the tower that once housed the wizard's chamber.

For a long moment, neither spoke. They simply stared at the object in silence.

"And Bethan said he used this to spy on us while we were in Zenobia?" Shani asked.

"Yes. It obviously has great power."

She reached out cautiously and placed her fingertips against Avoch-Dar's enchanted crystal. "It feels cold. Dead."

"But there may be some way of making it work again."

"How?"

He sighed. "I don't know."

"The thing might never come alive without the sorcerer's magic to power it. And even if you *can* make it work, what then?"

"I have no idea. But this crystal's the only link to him, and he has the book –"

"Which might restore your arm. I know. No one wants that more than me, Dalveen. But it's wise not to build your hopes too high. Avoch-Dar and that accursed book may never be seen again. Don't become obsessed."

"I'll try not to." He smiled. "And what do you intend doing now?"

"I've decided to move on."

He detected a hint of sadness in her voice. "I had hoped you might consider joining us here at Torpoint. I'm sure you could be helpful in a number of ways."

"Thanks, Dalveen. It's a tempting offer, but ... well, as I said, I'm still looking for my place in the world. I'm not ready to settle down just yet."

"I understand. Though I'll be sorry to see you go. But if your wanderings bring you back to Allderhaven..."

"Then I'll be seeing you, have no doubt on that score. And if you should ever need me, you only have to put out the word. Who knows, perhaps I'll even make it back for your wedding." She paused and held his gaze. "Whenever that might be."

"We're not sure yet. But you'd be an honoured guest, you know that. When were you thinking of leaving?"

"Right away. I don't believe in long goodbyes."

"I could wish it were not so soon. I'll miss you, Shani."

"And I you." She lifted her hand and lightly touched his cheek. "Farewell, Nightshade."

Then without further word she turned and left the chamber.

Dalveen Leandor sat pondering the mystery of Avoch-Dar's crystal until the sun rose on a new day.